Fennia's Secrets

Iván Shtanko Matosas

Dedicated to:
Mel, Ennedi, and Karsten,
To Xela and Bodhi.
To the memory of my mother, Rosa.
To Maria Alexandra.
To María José, whose love for books
inspired me to write one.
To Andrés, Gabriel, and their families.
To everyone who read me stories
and tales when I was a child.
To my father, Pedro.

With gratitude to:
Rafael, who insisted I finish and publish this book.
To Lorena C. Brown and Ani Palacios, for their
patience, help, and advice on writing my first novel.
and to María Inés Quevedo for her cover illustration.

Table of Contents

The Characters

Present-Day Figures

- **Víctor Cabot** – Photojournalist, investigator
- **Diana Díaz** – Spanish language teacher
- **Roberto González** – Director of *La Gaceta* newspaper
- **John McIntyre** – History professor, director of the Museum
- **Elizabeth McIntyre** – Wife of John McIntyre
- **Lieutenant James Wilkinson** – Police officer
- **The Smith and Ferguson Families**
  (Descendants of Annadee Bauer Fischer)
  - **Paul Smith** – Landowner
  - **Amelia Smith** – Wife of Paul, descendant of Annadee Bauer Fischer
  - **Ashley Smith** – Daughter of Paul and Amelia
  - **Antonina (Nina)** – Ashley's daughter
  - **David Ferguson** – Landowner, brother of Amelia, descendant of Annadee Bauer Fischer
  - **Caroline Ferguson** – Wife of David Ferguson

Historical Figures *(19th & Early 20th Century)*

- **Alexander Bauer** – Settler
- **Marie Anne Fischer** – Wife of Alexander
- **Annadee Bauer Fischer** – Daughter of Alexander and Marie Anne
- **Patrick Sans McGowan** – Sailor from *Elbe*

- **Karl Henning** – Sailor from *SMS Kielberg*
- **Hans Schneider** – Sergeant from *SMS Kielberg*

Supporting Character

- **Juan Ramírez** – Foreman of the *Neptuno* shipyard

Chapter I

February 10, 1832
Montevideo, Uruguay

She burst into the new offices of the Police Headquarters in an almost disrespectful manner. Her anguished mother accompanied her, but it was the young woman who spoke.

Her beauty and youth did nothing to hide the anger she felt toward herself and her mother, with whom she had clearly argued before entering. Her sky-blue eyes, glistening with unshed tears, filled with worry over the uncertainty that troubled her, searched among the officers for someone who could help her, give her hope, tell her that everything would be fine or, better yet, that he had already been there asking about her, looking for her. But that was not the case.

They had come to report the disappearance of her fiancé and to register their new residence, hoping that when he returned to Montevideo, he would know where to find her. The officer, indifferent despite noticing her hands tightly gripping the edge of the counter and her mother supporting her, simply dipped his pen in the inkwell, and wrote down what she said.

She repeated the process at the Port Captaincy of the young nation to ensure he knew she was waiting for him. No one could give her the answer she hoped for. No one had information about the situation on the islands, and no ships from there had arrived since the USS Lexington docked a week earlier. She knew she would wait for him her entire life and was certain he would come for her as soon as he could.

Every day, while she lived in Montevideo, she went to the dock to watch the ships arrive, asking passengers and officers if they had seen him or knew anything about his whereabouts. She sent letters to the last place they had been together, hoping to receive a reply one day.

Chapter II

1977
Paysandú, Uruguay

The shipyard foreman ignited the cutting torch and began carving an opening in the ship's hull. As he completed the final cut of a large rectangular section, Juan Ramírez let the heavy, rusted piece of metal drop onto the concrete of the dry dock floor, producing a dull thud and stirring up a cloud of dust that the wind quickly scattered. He wanted to create a more accessible entry point into the ship's interior before beginning the dismantling process.

The ninety-five-meter-long sailboat, built on the other side of the world in Le Havre, France, in 1902, was meeting its end in the city of Paysandú, Uruguay, seventy-five years later.

A hurricane in 1927 had snapped part of its masts, sealing its fate and marking the end of its voyages around the world. Yet, its true demise wouldn't begin until fifty years after that storm.

Done, Juan muttered. He turned off the torch, removed his goggles, and called out to the others, "Alright, boys, all set—get to work."

Juan had only been working at the shipyard for two years, but he was already overseeing all operations. Once the others had taken up their positions, he strolled through the ship, searching for a souvenir to add to his collection of naval artifacts.

It must have been magnificent to see this vessel sailing the open sea, he thought as he walked the length of the ship. Now, dull, dark, rusted, and on the verge of disappearing forever, it filled him with sadness. That's why he had the habit of taking something from each ship that ended its journey in his shipyard. After all, this was its final voyage, and someone had to honor it.

The old sailboat had been abandoned at the port of Montevideo ten years earlier, and anything of value it once held was long gone. Even so, Juan hoped that, with a bit of luck, he might find something to add to his collection and preserve a piece of its history.

After inspecting the ship from bow to stern, and just before stepping out empty-handed, he noticed something unusual wedged between the frames near the ceiling of the hold—something that didn't appear to be part of the ship. He furrowed his brow, looking for a way to reach it.

With the strength and agility of youth on his side, he climbed the beams until he was close enough. At once, he realized that whatever it was, it had been there for years, judging by its condition and the thick layer of accumulated dust. Now that the hold was better lit, thanks to the opening he had made, the object was visible. Whatever it might be, he decided it would become his souvenir from Fennia.

Balancing himself carefully, he clung to one of the frames and reached out, grasping the object. He gave it a gentle shake, sending a cloud of rusty dust tumbling heavily through the air, catching the golden morning light streaming into the hold. Only then did he realize—it was a simple wooden box.

Had it fallen from somewhere, or was it intentionally hidden? He wondered. *What could it be?*

He slipped the box into the pocket of his jacket and slid down the beams back to the floor. Once there, he dusted it off thoroughly and carefully pried it open. Inside, there was nothing but a single sheet of yellowed paper, folded into quarters.

He set the box on a beam and carefully unfolded the fragile paper. One detail stood out immediately: *27 Dezember 1939.* The rest of the handwriting, however, was difficult to decipher, as it was in a different language.

Not wanting to waste more time, he decided to examine it after his workday was done. He carefully placed the letter back into its original box, tucked it away with his tools, and went back to work.

That night, after all the workers had left the shipyard, Juan took the box to the workshop. He wiped it clean with a damp cloth, revealing the aged wood beneath years of dust and grime. Turning it over in his hands, he inspected every detail—the joints, the grain, the faint markings worn by time. Once again, he tried to make sense of the paper's writing and realized it was either German or a similar language.

Inside the lid, he noticed a faded label: *"Alpha Syringe."* Below it, a molded compartment held indentations shaped for a syringe and three needles.

It probably belonged to the ship's doctor, he thought, dismissing it without much further concern. *I'll have to find someone who can translate this for me.*

He placed the box in a cabinet alongside the other pieces in his collection and went home.

Work and other responsibilities began to pile up, delaying the translation. More ships arrived, bringing new projects, and Juan never found the time to have the letter translated. In the end, the box and its secret were forgotten once more, left to gather dust in a dark corner—waiting for someone else to uncover its truth.

Chapter III

2017
Paysandú, Uruguay

Víctor Cabot sat down for breakfast and his usual routine of reading the newspaper when the phone on the desk in the adjacent room began to ring.

Muttering a curse under his breath, he wondered if he should answer or just ignore it. He took a quick sip of his coffee, got up, and went to pick up the phone.

"Hello, good morning," he said, wiping a bit of coffee from the corner of his lips with his fingers.

"Good morning. Víctor?"

"Yes, that's me. Who's calling?"

"González. Roberto González... from *La Gaceta*."

Víctor had worked for the newspaper on several occasions, writing articles and taking photographs. It had been months since he'd last heard from *La Gaceta*, so the call was an unexpected surprise.

"Roberto! It's been a while!"

"Sure has. Time flies without us even noticing. Anyway, I thought you'd left the country, but yesterday someone told me you were still around."

"Yes, I'm still here. I just haven't been able to leave," he said, thinking of the many times his plans to move had been postponed for one reason or another. "It seems destiny doesn't want me to go."

"Destiny is unpredictable. It's hard to tell where it'll take us. But I'm glad you're still here because I need your help."

"Great! What can I do for you?" Víctor replied, his tone brightening.

"Could you go take some photos at the shipyard? They're for next Sunday's edition, but it's urgent."

"Urgent? Why? Did something happen?"

"No, nothing like that. It's for a special article about the old Korean fishing vessels docked there."

"Oh, those ships. I read in your paper that one of them caught fire last week."

"Yes, we still don't know what happened. It's a complete mystery."

"Strange, isn't it?"

"Very strange, Víctor. Anyway, none of my photographers are available this weekend, and this is urgent. Apparently, whether related to the fire or not, they'll begin dismantling the ships this Monday. So, could you photograph them before that happens?"

"Of course. No problem," Víctor replied without hesitation. Work had been scarce lately, and he needed to take any job that came his way.

"Do you want me to write the article, too?"

"No, I just need the photos. I already have all the details about the fire investigation, the ships' history, their construction, and everything else. Laura is working on the text. I only need the pictures before they start cutting the ships apart."

"Got it. No problem. You'll have them."

"And don't forget we need time for editing. You know how it is."

"Yes, Roberto, I know. Don't worry. You'll have your photos edited and ready by Monday at the latest."

"Great, thanks a lot. Do you have something to write with? I'll give you the contact information for the man in charge of the shipyard so you can coordinate with him."

Víctor grabbed a pencil from the desk, jotted the number down on a scrap of paper nearby, and, after a few more pleasantries, hung up.

He was pleased. The job was a welcome opportunity, and he had always been fascinated by those ships. They had been sitting abandoned in the shipyard for over two years, and now, at last, he would have the chance to see them up close.

He hurried through breakfast, leaving the newspaper half-read, and immediately called the shipyard. The phone rang for a very long time before someone picked up. A calm, measured voice answered—one that carried both wisdom and weariness. After a brief introduction, they arranged to meet the following morning at nine. The gate would be open, and he would be waiting in the office.

At dawn, Víctor was already awake. He prepared his *mate*, packed his camera and gear carefully into the car, and took a few slow sips of *mate* while mentally planning the shots he wanted to take. As the appointed time approached, he set off for the shipyard.

He arrived a few minutes early. Driving through the entrance, he passed beneath a faded, rusting sign whose letters were barely legible. The grounds stretched no more than a hectare, but the decay was unmistakable.

The grass was overgrown, the trees mostly dead, and the buildings bore the weary marks of time— paint peeling, windows grimy. Yet, the number of structures hinted at a past life, one of industry and purpose. It was clear that this place had once thrived. But those days were long gone.

Navigating carefully between two rust-streaked shipping containers, he passed a heap of corroded scrap metal nearly swallowed by weeds before arriving at the office, a squat building near a massive warehouse.

Beyond it, standing near the riverbank but firmly on dry land, the ships he had come to photograph loomed before him. They rested side by side like two enormous, slumbering beasts—forgotten giants awaiting their fate. A long ladder, secured to one of the hulls, stretched upward to the deck.

Sunshine and Adala 101. Former Korean fishing vessels. He knew little about them beyond what the newspaper had reported about the fire.

As he parked, a man emerged from the office carrying a thermos and a well-worn *mate*. A brown brindle dog followed at his heels, wagging its tail amicably.

"Good morning. You must be Mr. Ramírez, right?"

"Good morning. Yes, sir. Juan Ramírez, at your service," the man said, tucking the thermos under his arm as he extended his hand for a handshake, his grip firm and confident.

Ramírez had the look of an old sailor, a man who had spent more time around ships than on solid ground. Though he was no longer the shipyard foreman, he still came by often to catch up with old colleagues. Occasionally, he earned extra money as a night watchman.

"A pleasure, sir," Víctor replied. "This is the first time I've ever been inside the shipyard. I've always wanted to see it."

"Really? Well, here you are," Ramírez said with a faint smile. "Not that you've missed much. It's been a long time since this place was what it used to be. As you can see, everything's gone downhill."

"Back in the day, we built plenty of ships here, Mr. Cabot—fishing boats, small cargo carriers, sand dredgers. We repaired plenty, too. But those times are over. Now, all they do is dismantle whatever comes their way. Most ships are built in the capital these days—more market, more skilled labor."

He took a slow sip of *mate* before continuing.

"You know what's happening here, don't you? It's not just the shipyard. This whole town has gone downhill along with its industries. Paysandú It's not like it used to be," he said, a tinge of sorrow in his voice.

A sudden gust of wind stirred the eucalyptus trees lining the lot. Birds took flight, and a swirl of dust ghosted along the path, as if nature itself had come to mourn the past.

Juan turned his gaze toward the ships, poured himself another *mate*, and sighed deeply.

"Well, there they are. Waiting for their tragic end."

Víctor followed his gaze.

"That's right, Mr. Ramírez," he murmured.

The morning sun, still timid against the crisp autumn air, cast a muted ochre glow over the ships. Rust streaked their hulls like old wounds. Silent. Lifeless. Forgotten.

Juan Ramírez finished his *mate*, adjusting the bombilla without a word.

After a moment of quiet, Víctor finally broke the silence. "Ah… Anyway, Mr. Ramírez, since they're even bigger than I expected, I'd better get to work right away."

"Of course. You saw how to climb up, right?" Ramírez gestured toward the ladder. "There's a platform between the two decks—cross there if you need to move between the ships. If you need anything, just call out."

"No problem."

"Oh! You know one of them was set on fire not long ago, right?"

"Yes, I know. I read about it in the paper. You can still smell the burn a bit. Any news on that? What did the police say?"

"As far as I know, nothing. I guess they're still investigating. They say it was some *gurises*—you know, kids messing around, or maybe a homeless person—but I didn't see anyone that day. It's all a bit strange, you know? Anyway, don't worry—if there were any ghosts, they would've burned up already!" Juan joked.

It took Víctor a little over two hours to finish his work. He began by photographing the ships from the outside, then boarded them to capture images of the deck and interior. When he was done, standing at the stern of the last ship, he took advantage of the elevated view to snap a few photos of the surrounding area. From there, he could see the municipal beaches to the north, Caridad Island across the river with its magnificent sandy banks exposed by the low waters levels of the Uruguay River, and, in the middle of it all, several sailboats from the Paysandú Yacht Club gliding by, their sails billowing in the brisk *pampero* wind.

After snapping a few photos and just as he was about to climb down, something along the riverbank caught his attention. From there, he could see the remains of an enormous vessel. All that was left was the rib-like structure of the hull, which, due to the low water levels, was now partly visible, buried halfway in the mud next to what appeared to be a disused dock.

He took some photos of it, climbed down and went to the shore for a closer look. After inspecting it and taking more photos, he went looking for Juan Ramírez. Maybe he could satisfy his curiosity.

"All right, my friend, I'm done!" Víctor said as he rejoined Juan.

"I'm glad to hear that. I imagine you took plenty of photos," Juan replied.

"Plenty, indeed. I always prefer to take more than necessary—especially knowing these ships will be gone soon. There won't be another chance after that."

"True enough," Juan agreed.

"Tell me, Mr. Ramírez," said Víctor, turning and pointing toward the shoreline, "what ship are those remains on the coast from? It looks like it was quite large."

"Ah, you saw that? Yes, it certainly was. That used to be the *Fennia*—a huge sailing ship, beautiful in its day, at least from what it looked like when it arrived here. It made me really sad to cut it up and watch it disappear."

"Sad?"

"Well, yes, sad. It was a magnificent ship: four masts, ninety-five meters long... and well, that's all that's left of it now. Just that bit of the frame and a few scattered bits of metal lying around."

"What happened to it?"

"Nothing much—we just scrapped it. It was an old cargo vessel... and a sailing one, imagine that. They brought it here, towed all the way from the capital, floating along the river, of course. When it arrived, its masts were broken, bent; it was in terrible condition— rusty, with most of the deck planks rotted away. It was really bad. After a few years, we left it as it is now. Its entire hull was made of iron. I know some of the plates were turned into wood-burning stoves, and those are probably still around somewhere in the city... As for the rest, that part was left because of the concrete ballast. It was too much work to break through it and remove the remaining metal, so we left it there. Oh, and I think there's still a piece of the bowsprit by the warehouse."

Víctor looked at him, waiting for further explanation. When none came, he asked, "Bowsprit? What's that?"

"Oh yes, sorry—it's like a mast at the front of the ship, slanting forward, where the triangular sails—the jib or genoa—are attached. You know what I mean?"

"Yes... well, I think I understand. I have to admit, I don't know much about ships or their terminology. But I'd like to learn more about the *Fennia*. What happened to it? Where was it from, and how did it end up here?"

"Well, from what I remember and what I was told, it was built in France in the early 1900s. Many years later, in 1927, a storm at Cape Horn broke its masts. After that, it was never used again. As for how it got to Uruguay—well, that's a mystery to me. I do know it showed up in Montevideo in 1967 and was abandoned there. Then, in 1976, it was brought to Paysandú, and the following year, we started scrapping it."

Víctor did the math in his head and added, "That was forty years ago—about six years before I was even born."

"Time sure flies. Feels like it was just yesterday. I remember it clearly—we worked on that ship, and I was in charge back then. I also remember finding a box in its hold, with a letter inside dated... 1939, yes, 1939, if my memory serves me right. I should still have it somewhere. If you're interested, I could look for it and show it to you."

"Yes, absolutely! If you have it handy... I love antiques," Víctor replied eagerly.

"I never got around to looking into the ship, the box, or the letter. I had thought about getting it translated—it was written in another language,

German, I think—but time passed, and I kept putting it off. Eventually, I just left it. You know, I used to save things from the ships I dismantled—photos, papers, engine plates, anything unusual I found. Anyway, I was going to call a German guy I knew, but in the end, I never did."

"I see, Mr. Ramírez. So, you never found out what the letter said?"

"No, never."

"Well, I could help you with that if you like. Do you have any photos of the ship?"

"Not here, but I have some from when it arrived and during the dismantling. I can find them for you."

"Yes, that would be great. Thank you so much."

Víctor returned to his car, stored his equipment, and accompanied Juan to the shed. Ramírez offered to show him his entire collection of artifacts and ship parts. Víctor thanked him but explained that he didn't have much time that day—he needed to focus on editing his work. Still, he was eager to see the *Fennia's* box and the letter.

"Of course," Ramírez said, searching through an old wooden cabinet. "I think someone either hid or lost it on the ship, and that's how it ended up there. Now, the question is… where did I put it? Did I lose it myself?"

After rummaging through the pile of artifacts and parts he had accumulated over the years, he finally found it.

"Here it is," he said, blowing off a layer of dust. "From what you can see, it's an old syringe kit box, like the ones doctors used back in the day. Remember those? I don't know if they still use them—nowadays,

I think they're stainless steel. But inside, there was only a piece of paper—a letter, from what I can tell."

"Nothing else?"

"Nope," Ramírez replied. "Just the letter. The syringe and needles were already gone. And, like I said, I think it's in German."

Víctor examined the letter. Despite being nearly 80 years old, the paper was still in relatively good condition, though the writing had faded significantly.

"I can try to translate this for you, Mr. Ramírez. My curiosity has been sparked, and I'd be happy to do it after I finish my work for the newspaper."

"I'd be delighted, Mr. Cabot. Forty years have passed—I think it's time we finally learn what it says, don't you? You know what? I'll lend it to you. When you're done, bring it back and let me know what you find out, all right?"

Víctor thanked him and promised that once he had uncovered all the information about the letter and the *Fennia*, he would return for another chat—and to see the rest of the collection. They parted ways with a firm handshake.

Chapter IV

Investigation

After leaving the shipyard, Víctor went straight home to select and edit fifteen to twenty photos from the 350 he had taken before presenting them to the editor for final selection. That afternoon, feeling more at ease after wrapping up his editing work, he prepared some *mate*—his favorite drink, a traditional South American tea—lit the fireplace in the living room, and settled on the couch facing the fire. After a few sips of *mate*, he watched the flames dance and listened to the eucalyptus wood crackle. Then he pulled the *Fennia's* box from his backpack and set it on the table. Its scent carried hints of damp wood and oil, likely from years spent in the workshop's cabinet among other ship parts. Thinking it might make an interesting newspaper piece, he took photos of the box and letter. Perhaps it held historical value or, at the very least, could make for an interesting story.

He pulled out his notebook, jotting down details as he snapped pictures: *"Wooden box made of oak, bronze hinges, dimensions: 165 mm x 115 mm x 75 mm, bronze front latch."*

He opened the lid and noted its interior details as well. Gently, he took out the paper and carefully unfolded it on the table. The ink had faded so badly that the note was barely legible. It was dated December 27, 1939, and signed by someone named Karl Henning— or something along those lines.

He strained to make out more, but the words remained elusive.

Given the paper's age, Víctor decided to make a photocopy to prevent further deterioration and, hopefully, enhance the contrast of the faded letters.

He went to his office, adjusted the printer settings, placed the sheet on the scanner, and pressed "Print." As he had hoped, now the letters on the copy appeared sharper and easier to read. He returned to the living room to finish inspecting the box he had left by the fireplace before starting to translate the letter. Picking up the box, he closed the lid and turned it over, searching for any markings or clues on the bottom. As he did, he felt something shift inside. He opened the box again and gave it a gentle shake. The heat from the fire had dried out the wooden lining, causing it to loosen from the sides. Curious, he gently shifted the lining to see if anything was hidden beneath it until it came loose completely. The lining itself bore no markings, so he set it aside. But upon inspecting the interior, he found it odd that the bottom panel was much thicker than the sides. On closer inspection, he realized the panel was also loose. He retrieved the Swiss knife he always carried and carefully used one of its blades to pry up the edge, lifting it slightly. Flipping the box upside down, he tapped it lightly on the table. Suddenly, the wooden panel fell away, revealing a hidden compartment. To Víctor's astonishment, another aged, yellowed piece of paper tumbled out, folded into quarters. *Wow... what's this?* He muttered, eyes widening in surprise. He picked up the paper and unfolded it. It was a hand-drawn map, though faded and barely visible. Even with his knowledge of geography, Víctor couldn't place the map's location. It showed only the outline of a coastline, a few marks that seemed to represent hills or mountains, several bays or inlets, and a small town with its dock. *Could Ramírez have seen this?* Víctor wondered. *Hmm... he would've told me.*

What had seemed like nothing more than an antique syringe box with an old letter had just become a mystery. After photographing the box and noting down every detail that might aid his investigation, Víctor went to his desk, sank into his worn-out chair, and powered on his computer. He was eager to translate the letter and examine the map right away. Later, he would dig into everything he could uncover about the *Fennia*. He pulled up an online translator—the first he could find, as he'd never used one before. He considered calling a German-speaking friend—faster and easier—but using the computer felt more discreet. Besides, he disliked asking for favors and wasn't about to start now, especially for something that might be insignificant—or, on the contrary, something far too important to share just yet. He began typing each word exactly as it appeared in the letter. Relief washed over him at first—the words were simple enough to understand. But as the sentences unfolded into a story, unease crept in. It was a letter from a son to his parents, written at the start of World War II. He reassured them that he was safe and that they shouldn't worry—despite the fact that he had been captured and was now a prisoner of war. The only comfort was that he was alive and well. He described the sinking of his ship, the *SMS Kielberg*, and how only he and Sergeant Hans Schneider had made it out alive. He mentioned that they were in good health, being treated well, and that he missed his family deeply.

He explained that he couldn't reveal his location or share more information, as all letters were censored. The British were monitoring every word, and if he disclosed anything deemed confidential, his letter would never be sent. However, he mentioned that they were being moved—far from the war in Europe. That, at least, was good news. But again, he couldn't say where.

The letter ended with a heartfelt plea for his family to stay safe. He reassured them that when he returned to Germany, they would never have to worry about anything again. Confidently, he declared that the war would be brief and promised he would be back with them soon.

Finally, he bid farewell to his little sister, Helga, and sent his love to his parents.

Chapter V

December 21, 1939
South Atlantic

It was late afternoon when sergeant Hans Schneider of the German destroyer *SMS Kielberg* sat on the overturned keel of the slowly sinking ship. Dazed by the recent battle, the destruction, and the death closing in around him, he held onto the hope that the enemy destroyer would arrive in time to rescue the survivors. A few remaining men desperately tried to climb onto the slippery hull, but one by one, they succumbed to hypothermia or their injuries. Unfortunately, he also realized that when the ship disappeared under the surface of the frigid waters, he would meet the same end.

The battle and the war were over for him; his mind no longer dwelled on them. His sole focus now was survival.

The enemy destroyer that had defeated them was approaching, fueling his optimism—surely, they would rescue him. But then, without warning, it changed course, turned to starboard, and sailed away. Perhaps they feared enemy submarines, or maybe they thought no one was left alive. Whatever the reason, no rescue was coming. His fragile hope began to fade.

He felt the vibrations of the cold metal beneath his feet and the rush of air escaping in bursts from the twisted steel. Meanwhile, the desperate cries for help from his comrades grew fainter and fainter

Do miracles exist? he wondered. *Would it matter if I prayed now and repented for my sins?*

He still had his pistol. He felt it, gripped it in his hand, and thought about using it to end his agony, but he couldn't. In the whirlwind of a thousand thoughts racing through his mind, his wife and family appeared. They would never know what had happened to him or how he died. He couldn't stop fighting, couldn't give up, but he had no choice—what else was there to do?

Minutes passed, and the cries of his comrades faded away until he realized he was the last one.

The sun had already set, and in the growing twilight of the advancing night, he spotted a white boat in the distance. *Could I swim to it? Would I make it? Would I have the strength? Could I endure the cold?* he wondered.

He cupped his hands around his mouth to direct his voice and shouted with all his might:

"Hey! Is anyone on the boat? Hey!" he shouted desperately.

Seconds passed in silence. He called out again, his voice now edged with panic. Just as he was about to plunge into the frigid water to try to reach it, a voice responded:

"Yes! Where are you?"

"Here, on the stern!" he exclaimed. "Yes, here! Here!" He waved his arms frantically.

I'm saved, he thought.

The nearly full moon had just begun its ascent on the horizon, casting a pale glow over the shattered remains of the ship. Its light reflected off his soot-streaked white uniform as he sat on the gleaming hull of the doomed vessel, now taking its final breaths.

"Okay, I see you! I'm coming!" the sailor called out. "Who are you?"

"Schneider, Sergeant Hans Schneider. And you?"

"*Matrose* Karl Henning, *Herr* Sergeant."

Karl rowed the boat closer, the oars slicing through the dark water. Hans braced himself, then leaped into the boat, his body trembling from exhaustion and cold. As the boat rocked beneath him, he let out a shaky breath.

He was alive.

"Let's get out of here. The ship doesn't have much time left," he shouted.

Together, they rowed quickly until they reached a safe distance. Once far enough away, they stopped and watched as their ship vanished beneath the waves forever. Then, silence reigned.

They searched the area, calling out into the night, lifting motionless bodies in the desperate hope of finding someone still alive. But there was no one. Nothing left to do.

Karl exhaled heavily. "Looks like it's just us, Sergeant. I'm sorry."

Hans swallowed hard, his throat tight. "Yes... me too." He drew a shaky breath before nodding. "It's all right. At least you saved my life—I owe you for that. Thank you."

They both knew the truth. Staying any longer was pointless. No rescue was coming.

"What do we do now, Herr Sergeant?"

"Hans. My name is Hans. After all, I owe you my life—no more formalities."

"Very well, Hans. Do you know where we are?"

"Not really. It was a secret mission; they didn't give us any information. But I think I saw some islands earlier this afternoon," he said, searching for direction among the constellations before pointing westward.

"That way," he reiterated once he was certain. "It's possible it's enemy territory, but we'll go there—we have no other choice."

And so, they began rowing, keeping their course guided by the stars. After a couple of hours, just as their hopes began to fade, they spotted the dark silhouette of mountains rising beneath the starry sky in the distance. Life, it seemed, was offering them another chance.

As they approached, they saw the white sands of a beach glinting under the moonlight and decided to head there to land. Without knowing where they were or whether the coast was defended or patrolled, they proceeded in silence.

When the boat slid onto the sand, pushed by the strong waves, they jumped out and dragged it further inland. Then, crouching down, they stayed still for a while, scanning for any movement. But nothing happened. Only then did they move the boat against the nearest cliff and set up a makeshift camp to shield themselves from the wind and cold.

Now, the only sounds were the wind and the endless rhythm of the waves breaking on the beach.

The explosions and the screams of their comrades were behind them, and they felt lucky to be there, in their modest hideout—wet, cold, but alive.

At dawn, Hans woke up. He nudged Karl in the back to wake him up. It was possible that the British Royal Navy patrolled the area, so they needed to leave the beach as soon as possible. They had to find a safer place to hide and search for water and food. The boat contained some emergency rations, but it wasn't much. In addition to that, there were a pair of binoculars, a flashlight, a roll of rope, and a knife. They camouflaged the boat among the rocks, covered it with bushes, grabbed the supplies, and headed inland.

The day, despite the persistent wind, was pleasant, with clear skies and good visibility— something both beneficial and problematic, as they could be seen from far away, but for the moment, however, no ships were in sight.

The beach was wide, crescent-shaped, nestled between two hills. Once they reached the top of the dune, they could finally see the vastness of the area. There were no houses, no roads, and no trees—only grass and bushes no taller than their knees. The terrain sloped gently from the coastline, with a few hills and mountains in the distance. Nearby, cows and sheep grazed peacefully, which suggested that someone tended them and likely lived in the area.

They mulled over their options for a few moments and decided to head for one of the nearby mountains. It seemed like the best place to hide, survey their surroundings, and plan their next move. Staying near the coast was out of the question. "The further inland, the better," they told themselves.

By the time they reached the summit of the nearest mountain two hours later, the breeze had dried their clothes. They built a small shelter and settled between the rocks, relieved to have reached a temporary haven. After a moment, Hans took the binoculars and began scanning the area. From their vantage point, they had a broad view of the surrounding landscape of this huge island. Suddenly, as Hans swept his gaze across the desolated terrain, he spotted, far to the west, a small village or hamlet. The red-roofed, white-walled houses stood out against the dry green of the fields.

"There are houses to the west, Karl!"

"That's great—there are people here then! We can get help!" Karl said, his tone hopeful.

"Not so fast, young man," Hans replied, laughing. "Did you forget this might be enemy territory? They could be the same people who sank us. We have no idea who lives there or what they think of us. It's better if they don't know we're here."

Looking more closely, Hans swore under his breath. In one of the house windows, there was an English flag. It was now obvious they couldn't seek any kind of help. After a moment, he handed the binoculars to Karl and said:

"Look behind the shed, above the roof. Doesn't that look like a mast?"

"Yes, it does… and it's moving. It's on the water."

"Yes, that's what I think. Looks like a sailboat."

"But what are you planning to do? We just came from the sea. Do you want to go back out there?

Where do you think we'll go? Can't you see we're in the middle of nowhere?"

"Yes, Karl, but I don't think we'll ever be safe on this island. I know we passed near Tierra del Fuego two days ago. The Argentine coast must be close to the west. We can try to get there."

"Do you think that's possible?" Karl asked, astonished.

"I have a sailboat back in Laboe, I know what I'm talking about. I've navigated long distances. I can do it."

"Alright then," Karl said with a shrug. "We can try."

"Yes, and the sooner we leave the island, the better. For now, let's stay here and rest. It'll be best to wait until nightfall to take the sailboat."

"Look," Karl said, pointing to a peak closer to the village. "You see that hill? I think it'd be better to go there. It's closer, and we'd have a better view. From there, it'll be quicker to reach the boat during the night. Don't you agree?"

"Good idea, young man. I hadn't thought of that. Let's eat something now and get some rest."

Hours later, still with no ships or patrols in sight, they decided to head for the other hill. They felt confident no one knew they were there but were determined not to stay long.

Moving with more caution now that they were near the village, their walk took longer.

After about three hours, they were in their new position—right at the top of the hill, about two kilometers north of the village.

"What do you think, Hans? It doesn't look like there's anyone there—no movement, no smoke from the chimneys, no animals in the pens. Could it be a trap?" Karl asked uneasily.

"No, I don't think so. How could they possibly know we're here?" the sergeant replied confidently, trusting in their luck.

But suddenly, as Hans scanned the horizons with the binoculars, he spotted a destroyer near the beach where they had landed.

"Damn it!" he exclaimed, immediately ducking behind the rocks. "They're probably searching for bodies or any survivors. No movements, Karl. I don't think they know we're here, and it needs to stay that way. With some luck, maybe they won't notice our boat. If they move on, we'll take that sailboat tonight and get off this island. By morning, we'll be far from here."

The village appeared abandoned. There were no vehicles visible anywhere. After a while, they saw the destroyer slowly continue its course until it disappeared over the horizon.

Before night fell, they prepared a plan. From the summit, they spotted an animal trail that wound through the grasses and ended at the pens of the village. That would be the path they followed. If all went well, they would board the sailboat, inspect it to ensure it was seaworthy, and if it checked out, they would leave immediately. If not, they would find whatever they needed to make it safe, even if it took a few days. They didn't want to risk another shipwreck or suffer hardship at sea. The moon, which would rise later, would illuminate their trek.

Chapter VI

2017
Paysandú, Uruguay

Poor man, how naive, thought Víctor as he finished reading the letter. *He could have never imagined at that moment that the war would drag on for nearly six more years. What happened to them? Did they survive the war?*

But why hadn't this letter been sent? What happened? And what was it doing in that box on a ship in Paysandú? According to Juan Ramírez, it was a cargo sailboat, not a warship. And besides, if it stopped sailing in 1927, what happened between that year and 1939? Where was it? Why was a letter written in 1939 there? he wondered.

The more he thought about it, the more questions arose.

And why hide the map? Could it be that it marked the place where they were imprisoned?

He picked up the drawing again and examined it carefully. It didn't look familiar to him at all. The only clear features were the hills or mountains, some houses, and a port. Three bays were sketched, but it didn't resemble Montevideo at all, where the *Fennia* had been before being towed to Paysandú.

Montevideo only has one big hill, not several, like in the drawing. And the village and port seemed far too small to be the capital of Uruguay in 1939, he thought, quickly dismissing that possibility.

He also knew that the *Fennia* wasn't in Montevideo when the German battleship *Graf Spee* arrived in December of 1939. But... could there still be a connection between these two ships?

He translated the words on the drawing, but they offered little help. They weren't place names, only geographical features: hill, mountain, stream, lagoon, bay, island, village. No names, no compass directions, no scale or measurements. No latitude, no longitude. Nothing.

Well, this isn't very useful, he muttered, leaning back in his chair as he poured himself another *mate. It looks like whoever made this drew it for themselves— just enough to remember the place, but meaningless to anyone else if it fell into the wrong hands.*

After considering all the possibilities, he picked up the paper again and placed it under the lamp for closer inspection. He retrieved a magnifying glass from his desk drawer and examined every small detail, focusing on a faint stain near the base of the drawing.

It might just be natural wear from age... but what if it's something more? he thought

To test his theory, he ran the map through the photocopier, adjusting the contrast—just as he had done with the letter.

When the copy emerged, something unexpected appeared.

Within the stain, now clearer, he could make out an X—and beneath it, names: Patrick Sans McGowan and, just below that, something resembling Liberty Rose.

"Aha! Something's here," he murmured, his pulse quickening. "But what? Could these be places names?"

With both the drawing and letter translated, Víctor turned his attention to researching the *Fennia*, the *SMS Kielberg*, and whatever—or whoever— *Liberty Rose, Karl, Hans, and Patrick* might be.

If he could uncover more about the *Fennia*, he might learn which ports it had visited and which routes it had traveled. That could help him match the map to a specific location and finally determine what part of the world it depicted.

His initial online search led him through countless ships bearing the same name—different types, different eras—yet none seemed to have ended up in Paysandú. He sifted through maritime archives, ship registries, and historical documents, following thread after thread, until finally, something promising appeared.

On a maritime history website, he found a *Fennia* that matched his search. The description, accompanied by two photographs of a massive four-masted sailing ship, read:

"FENNIA. Steel-hulled vessel with a barque rig of four masts, built in 1902 at the Chantiers de la Méditerranée shipyard in Le Havre, France (hull no. 265) for the Société des Long Courriers Français of Le Havre, under the name CHAMPIGNY. Its dimensions

were 312.0 x 45.0 feet (95.10 x 13.70 meters) with a register of 3,200 tons.

On May 26, 1906, it sustained damage after colliding with the Chilean barque NELSON and the British steamer MADURA during departure maneuvers in Valparaíso.

In 1916, it was sold to the Société Générale d'Armement of Nantes, France.

In 1922, it was laid up in the Canal de la Martinière.

In 1923, it was sold to the Finnish company Aktiebolaget Finska Skolkeppsrederiet of Helsingfors, Sweden, as a training ship and renamed FENNIA, replacing the first FENNIA (ex-GOODRICH).

Under Captain Christerson, while en route from Cardiff with a coal cargo destined for Valparaíso, it suffered severe damage during a force-ten storm on May 3, 1927, while attempting to round Cape Horn. It had to dock in the Falkland Islands for repairs. It was eventually decommissioned and served as a pontoon for the Falkland Islands Company.

During World War II, it was used as a detention center for German prisoners.

In 1966, it was acquired by the Maritime Museum of San Francisco.

In 1967, it was towed to Montevideo, where it was ultimately abandoned by its new owners."

If this ship was abandoned in Montevideo, perhaps it's not the same one, he thought. He needed to gather more information to be sure it was the same vessel.

Fortunately, his next search yielded details that clarified its fate. According to this source, that very same *Fennia*, after roughly ten years of neglect in Montevideo, was towed to Paysandú with the intention of being repaired. However, it was eventually dismantled at the local shipyard.

He no longer had any doubt that this was the ship he had been looking for. Furthermore, the information that it had been used to hold German prisoners in the Falkland Islands provided a clue as to why the letter was aboard the ship.

This detail made it almost certain that the letter and the map belonged to a German prisoner from World War II who had been detained on that vessel.

This was the first time Víctor had seen what the ship once looked like. One photo captured it in all its splendor—sails fully extended, curved by the wind. The other showed it anchored in Stanley, the capital of the Falkland Islands. Víctor could hardly believe that the rusted iron remains, now half-buried in the mud along the banks of the Uruguay River, were all that was left of such a magnificent vessel. *A ship like this should have ended up in a museum,* he thought. Now, he fully understood the sadness Juan Ramírez had felt while dismantling it.

In his search for information on these ships, Víctor discovered that several Nazi German vessels had been seized, confiscated, or sunk along the coasts of Argentina, Brazil, and Uruguay. Among them were the *Carl Fritzen, Ussukuma, Kielberg*, and the infamous pocket battleship *Graf Spee*. The latter was the most well-known in Uruguay, having anchored in Montevideo after a fierce battle with the British Royal Navy. Severely damaged, the *Graf Spee* sought refuge in the Uruguayan capital, but when the government denied permission for repairs, its crew scuttled the ship in the Río de la Plata on December 17, 1939.

As he dug deeper, Víctor read that the crews of the first two ships had been transported to the Falkland Islands aboard HMS *Cumberland*, assigned to the 2nd Cruiser Squadron Force G, the South American Division in 1939. After spending some time there, and due to issues with food and clothing, they were eventually relocated to South Africa in December 1939 or early 1940, also aboard HMS *Cumberland*.

Well, well, I think I'm getting closer to uncovering something here. This is starting to take shape, he thought, his pulse quickening.

Following another round of searches, Víctor came across an official webpage containing something truly intriguing—photocopies of letters and records from the Falkland Islands authorities during World War II. These were official documents: correspondence, telegrams, prisoner lists, credit notes, payments, maintenance records, and more.

And there it was. The *Fennia* was mentioned multiple times.

Among the documents, he found an extensive list of names of those who had been held aboard the ship. His eyes scanned the list until they landed on two familiar names—*Hans Schneider, 35, and Karl Henning, 18.*

But there was no mention of *Patrick Sans McGowan* or *Liberty Rose.*

Frowning, Víctor turned his attention to the SMS Kielberg, searching for any details that might shed more light on its fate. What he found was frustratingly sparse—too sparse. It was listed as a

German Type 1936A destroyer from World War II, recorded as missing and presumed sunk by the British Royal Navy early in the war near the Falkland Islands. Built by AG Weser in Bremen, Germany, it measured 125 meters in length, 12 meters in width, and had a displacement of 2,450 tons. It carried five 150mm guns, torpedo launchers, and depth charges.

That was it. No additional records, no reports, no crew logs.

Víctor leaned back, rubbing his chin. *Strange...* It struck him as odd that so little information existed on this particular vessel. Could it have been lost in the chaos of war? Or deliberately erased to conceal certain missions?

His mind circled back to the map. The names *Patrick Sans McGowan* and *Liberty Rose* had to mean something. A location? A port? A hidden reference?

Fueled by curiosity, he pulled up Google Maps and typed in both names. Nothing. Not a single result.

He exhaled sharply, staring at the screen. *So what am I missing?*

What if Liberty Rose was a warship? Víctor wondered.

He searched through the same websites where he had found information about the *Fennia*, but once again, he came up empty-handed.

Through the silence of the night, the bells of the nearby basilica rang three times, marking the hour. Time had slipped away unnoticed, each tick of the clock echoing louder in Víctor's mind. Frustration settled in. This was turning into a far longer investigation than he'd anticipated.

He got up, stretched, and made himself a strong coffee to keep his eyes from closing. As he sipped, he ran through everything he had uncovered so far, trying to piece it all together.

Just a little longer, he thought, his resolve solidifying. He sat back down, cracked his knuckles, and resumed his search.

This time, he typed both names—Patrick Sans McGowan and *Liberty Rose*—together into the search engine. To his surprise, a page about Uruguayan history appeared, featuring an article from 1832. His fingers hovered over the keyboard, heart pounding as he read the headline.

The article detailed the disappearance of a man born in the *Banda Oriental* in 1812—Patrick Sans McGowan.

Aha! Víctor muttered to himself, pulse quickening as he scrolled down the page.

According to the article, Sans McGowan had found a frigate stranded on the *Islas Malvinas* near Volunteer Point under the name *Liberty Rose*. This discovery supposedly took place in December 1831.

A 19-year-old ranch worker from Montevideo, Sans McGowan claimed to have discovered the ship, but when authorities arrived to investigate, the ship had mysteriously vanished overnight. There was no wreck to confiscate, no trace of the vessel left behind, and so the case was deemed unresolved. What was even stranger was that Sans McGowan himself had disappeared just a few weeks later—on January 22, 1832—right before he was set to return to Montevideo. The report itself had been submitted by Annadee Bauer Fischer, an 18-year-old from Montevideo, who was

Patrick's fiancée at the time and a former resident of the *Islas Malvinas*—specifically *Puerto Soledad*. She had arrived in Montevideo a week earlier aboard the USS Lexington. *Wait... these are the same names from the drawing!* Víctor's heart raced. *I found them! This is it!* He leaned forward, eyes scanning the screen, but his excitement quickly turned to a cold, gnawing feeling. His mind went back to Karl Henning's drawing—the one dated more than a hundred years after the events he was reading about.

How is that possible? Víctor thought, brows furrowed.

More than a hundred years had passed between Karl Henning's drawing and the disappearance of Patrick Sans McGowan, not to mention the *Liberty Rose* incident. A full 107 years.

Could they be connected? Víctor's thoughts raced. *Why would Karl Henning mention someone who vanished a century earlier? How did he even know about him?*

The realization hit him like a wave, but the mystery was only deepening. At least now, Víctor had a clearer direction. He had uncovered who Patrick Sans McGowan was, what the *Liberty Rose* might be, and why they were intertwined in this puzzle.

One thing was now certain—the answer seemed to lie in a single location: the Falkland Islands.

The *Fennia*, Patrick Sans McGowan, Annadee Bauer Fischer, the *Liberty Rose*, the *SMS Kielberg*, Hans Schneider, and Karl Henning—these names were now bound together by time and place, all connected to the same enigmatic piece of history, though separated by the years.

Then, like a bolt of lightning, it hit him.

Wait a minute! How could I be so stupid? That map—it must be of the islands!

Now all he had to do was find a spot on the islands that matched the drawing.

Ha! That should be easier now! Víctor thought.

But it wasn't that simple.

He opened Google Maps and zoomed in on the Falkland Islands. Most of the mountain ranges ran longitudinally. Comparing them to Karl's drawing, he determined that the bay in the sketch was oriented east-west. That meant he could immediately rule out Port Stanley's bay, where the *Fennia* had once been anchored—the geography didn't match at all.

There were still many possible locations, but little by little, his search narrowed.

Then another thought crept in.

Should I just go there?

It was tempting. A trip to the islands could make for a great article, maybe even an extended stay. But then he hesitated.

Is this story really worth it?

Another war had already scarred these latitudes—the Falklands conflict of 1982. Compared to that, the events of 1832 and 1939 seemed almost insignificant. Yet, the deeper Víctor dug, the more his curiosity grew.

He had to know. What had really happened? What was the meaning of the drawing? And why had it been hidden?

This feels important... even if, for now, it's just a mystery.

As dawn broke, exhaustion weighed heavily on him, but he had one last task before resting. He needed to drop off his photographs at the newspaper office. At least that would be one thing off his plate.

Besides, it was a good excuse to poke around. Maybe someone there had heard something, or perhaps the archives held a forgotten clue. If not, he'd head home, get some sleep, maybe, and then return to unravel the mystery of the *Fennia*.

At the newspaper office, Víctor handed in his work and took the opportunity to ask around. Did anyone remember anything? Have they ever heard of *Fennia*?

No luck.

With no leads, his only option was to search the archives.

But even that seemed like a long shot. If there were any articles, they'd likely be about the ship itself—not whatever had been hidden in its hold. Worse yet, the newspaper had no digital archive. He'd have to sift through old editions, page by page—a painstaking process that could take hours, if not days.

Víctor sighed. He didn't have the patience for that. Not right now.

For the moment, the best course of action was to head home and dig deeper into his own investigation.

When Víctor arrived home, he prepared a fresh *mate* and settled at his desk, a quiet confidence settling over him. The riddle was there, waiting to be unraveled—and he was certain he could find the answer.

He powered up his computer, and the map of the Falkland Islands immediately filled the screen.

"Alright, let's see what we can find," he murmured, rubbing his hands together for warmth.

Carefully, he placed Karl's map on the desk and traced every detail onto a transparent sheet of paper. With steady hands, he placed the overlay against his computer screen, adjusting it meticulously, aligning landmarks and coastlines, searching for the key that would unlock its secrets.

After a while, a pattern emerged. Several sites stood out—not perfect matches, but close enough. Byron Bay, Old House Bay, White Rock Bay, King George Bay, Berkeley Sound, and Choiseul Sound— all east-west-oriented bays.

This is getting better, he thought.

The list of possible locations was shrinking. Now, he just needed to figure out which of these places Karl Henning or Hans Schneider—or both—had been in.

"Wait a second", he muttered, studying the map more closely. "What about the *Liberty Rose*? Where did the note say it ran aground? Could it be one of these places?"

Víctor revisited the open pages mentioning Patrick's discovery of a ship. Perhaps he had missed something.

"Let's see… Here it is! According to this note, it was near… Volunteer Point. Okay, let's find where that is."

In his research on the history of the ships and the islands, Víctor discovered that during the time Patrick Sans McGowan supposedly found the *Liberty Rose*, significant events had unfolded on the island. Though he couldn't be certain, he suspected that the arrival of the U.S. war frigate *USS Lexington* at Port Louis/*Puerto Soledad* in December 1831—and the subsequent destruction of the settlement by its crew—was somehow connected to the story. Adding to the intrigue, Annadee Bauer Fischer had traveled aboard that very same ship to Montevideo, arriving on February 3, 1832, where she, a week later, reported her fiancé's disappearance. According to her account, the *Liberty Rose* had run aground in December 1831.

Víctor wasn't entirely sure what had happened in the Falkland Islands during that time, but one thing was certain—Annadee and Patrick had been there when it unfolded.

When Víctor located Volunteer Point on the map, he realized it lay at the entrance to one of the seven bays that closely resembled Karl's drawing—Berkeley Sound, also known as Bahía de la Anunciación or San Luis, depending on the era or map consulted.

As he studied the sketch, trying to match the bays and coastlines, he instinctively rotated it. Then, something clicked. By flipping Karl's map upside down, the contours of the coastline, the hills, and the settlement aligned almost perfectly.

"Hey, hey!" Víctor shouted, excitement surging through him. "It's here! It has to be here!"

Had Karl drawn the map upside down on purpose? Or had he simply been disoriented when sketching it?

But one mystery remained: the *X* on the map wasn't placed where the *Liberty Rose* had supposedly run aground. Instead, it was somewhere inland.

Víctor scoured the internet for more information about the people connected to the mystery, but he came up empty-handed. The historical records only mentioned major events and prominent figures in the Falkland Islands. There was nothing more about Patrick Sans McGowan, Annadee Bauer Fischer, or the *Liberty Rose*. Nor did he find anything beyond a brief mention of the supposed prisoners, Hans Schneider and Karl Henning—their names appearing only on the list.

I have to go to the islands, he thought. *There's no other way to find out more. Someone there must know something.*

Despite his progress, questions kept circling in his mind, unsettling him: *How did Karl know about Patrick Sans McGowan in 1939 when Patrick had vanished in 1832? How did he even know his name? What had happened—and why had he included him in the drawing? And most importantly... what was the drawing pointing to? What was out there?*

There was no more he could do from behind a screen. Now, he was certain: he needed to take that trip.

But there was one problem—he didn't have the money.

As exhaustion finally pulled him under, his last thought before going to bed was about how he could afford to go.

Chapter VII

The Mystery of Patrick

Upon waking up with a clearer mind, Víctor realized it would be wiser to call the islands first. Before spending time and money chasing a ghost—or a story that might already be solved—he needed to find out what was already known.

Maybe this isn't a mystery at all, and here I am imagining strange things, he thought, chuckling to himself.

Not knowing anyone in the Falkland Islands, he decided to start with the local police. Perhaps they could point him in the right direction. A quick search online led him to the phone number of the Stanley police station, and without hesitation, he dialed.

A voice answered, and Víctor introduced himself as a Uruguayan journalist writing about the Falkland Islands. He kept it vague, mentioning only that he was looking for information about a person who had disappeared there in 1832. No need to reveal too much—he had no idea what kind of trouble this investigation might stir up.

The officer on duty, Lieutenant James Wilkinson, seemed caught off guard by such an unusual inquiry. Víctor couldn't tell if he was skeptical or merely surprised, but after a brief pause, the lieutenant responded politely.

"I'm afraid I don't have any information on something that old," he admitted. "A case from 1832 wouldn't even be in our archives. But…" He hesitated before continuing, "if anyone might know, it would be Professor John McIntyre. He's the secondary school history teacher and also the director of the local museum. If there's any record of that name or event, he's your best bet. Let me give you his number."

Víctor quickly jotted down the number. "Thank you, Lieutenant. I really appreciate it."

"No problem," Wilkinson replied. "Hope you find what you're looking for."

As soon as he hung up, Víctor wasted no time—he immediately dialed the professor's number.

As soon as Professor John McIntyre picked up, Víctor introduced himself just as he had with the lieutenant and got straight to the point. This time, he had better luck. McIntyre actually knew about the case.

"The mystery of Patrick?" McIntyre asked, sounding surprised. "Of course. I personally researched his disappearance years ago, but I never found anything conclusive. My investigation remains unfinished."

The professor went on to explain that Patrick's disappearance had been the subject of many rumors—some claimed he died during the attack on Port Louis, while others believed he left the islands with a treasure recovered from a shipwreck. But none of it was officially recorded, and no evidence had ever surfaced.

Search efforts continued for years, yet Patrick simply vanished.

Víctor thanked him for the information and explained that he was deeply interested in writing about the story. He was planning a trip to the Falkland Islands and would love to meet him in person to discuss it further.

"Of course, Mr. Cabot," McIntyre said warmly. "I'd be delighted to meet you and share everything I have on him. Do you have any idea when you'll be arriving?"

"Not yet, but hopefully soon," Víctor replied.

"Very well, very well. Before we end this conversation, may I ask how you found out about this case? It's not exactly a well-known story."

Víctor hesitated for a split second. "Ah... no, I don't mind. The internet," he said, keeping it vague. "These days, you can find anything online... well, almost anything."

"I see," McIntyre said, his tone unreadable. "Very well, then. I'll be waiting for you, Mr. Cabot."

They said their goodbyes, and Víctor hung up, feeling more eager than ever.

Knowing the story was real and the mystery remained unsolved only fueled his determination to make the trip. He had a strong feeling that the information he uncovered would finally reveal the truth. Was this what the hidden map pointed to? Could Karl and Hans have learned something about Patrick? What had happened there—or what was hidden at that location? Could the map actually mark the site of the rumored treasure Patrick was believed to have found?

Wasting no more time, and convinced that he was on the verge of solving Patrick's disappearance with *Fennia's* long-held secret, Víctor called the editor-in-chief of *La Gaceta*. He was certain Roberto González would be interested in the story—and might even help cover the cost of the trip.

However, he knew he had to convince him without revealing too much—especially about the possible existence of a treasure. It wasn't that Víctor wanted it for himself; he simply wanted to uncover the truth and surprise the world with his discovery. Besides, he had seen enough movies to know that talking too much always led to trouble. And he wasn't about to let that happen to him.

Roberto listened carefully as Víctor laid out his pitch. It was interesting, sure—but not compelling enough to justify an investigation, let alone sending someone all the way to the Falkland Islands.

From a numbers standpoint, it seemed like a costly, irrelevant pursuit. It wasn't a recent event, nor was it directly tied to Uruguay. Most concerning, there was no guarantee the trip would yield anything valuable. If others had searched before and come up empty, what were the odds Víctor would succeed?

What Víctor didn't mention was the map—the key piece that might tie everything together. He wasn't ready to share that yet, unsure of what he'd find at the marked location or if it would mean anything at all. Instead, he focused on Hans's letter from *Fennia's* box and Patrick's disappearance.

"Look, Roberto, let's do this. I have a gut feeling about it—something tells me I need to investigate this, and I can't explain why. The story is much bigger and more intriguing than it seems."

Víctor wasn't making that up. He truly believed it.

"You could publish it in stages, like a serialized piece. I'm sure readers would love it, especially since it involves a ship that ended up on our shores. You're a fan of maritime stories, aren't you?"

Roberto sighed. "Yeah, I am. But… are you holding something back, Víctor?"

Víctor didn't answer. He didn't want to.

Roberto chuckled. "I thought so. You know more than you're letting on, but you're not going to spill it, are you?"

"Look, all I'm asking for is your support. Let's make this happen," Víctor said, dodging the question.

Roberto considered it. The story had potential, but sending someone to the Falklands wasn't like covering a local event. It was a real commitment.

"Fine," he finally said. "I trust you. I'm taking a risk, but you better bring me something substantial. We need a real story—something that sells. I think you've got something here, and knowing you, I'm confident you'll deliver. You have one week. That's all I can give you. I don't want to lose money on this. Got it?"

Although Víctor often second-guessed himself, this was not the moment for doubt. One week would have to be enough. It was better than nothing.

"Thanks, Roberto. Don't worry. I'll stop by your office later to sort out the details. See you soon."

Hanging up, Víctor felt a surge of excitement. Without wasting a second, he called his travel agent to book the flight.

The agent laughed. "So, you're finally heading back to the U.S.?"

Víctor grinned. "No, no! Change of plans… again."

After a brief explanation, the agent checked the schedule. "Next available flight is Saturday, June 24."

"Perfect," Víctor said. That gave him nearly three weeks to prepare.

Chapter VIII

First Day in the Islands

As the plane broke through the clouds, Víctor squinted through the window, hoping to catch a glimpse of the rugged coastline below. His eyes traced the distant outlines of jagged cliffs and rolling hills as he searched for Port Louis and the area he planned to explore. But within seconds, a thick mist swallowed the view, leaving him frustrated. All he could do now was hope for better luck in the days ahead.

The landing was a bit rough at first, but they touched down safely. Víctor let out a sigh of relief, grateful to be safely on the ground. He hated flying and avoided it whenever possible, only boarding a plane when there was no other option.

As he stepped out of the cabin and onto the stairs leading to the tarmac, a sharp, icy wind slashed across his face. At that moment, he questioned his decision to embark on this journey in the depths of the southern hemisphere's winter. But the promise of discovery—the chance to unearth what had been hidden for many years—drove him forward. The relentless gusts, mixed with freezing drizzle and drifting snowflakes, stole his breath away, stirring memories of his first winter in New York—his first encounter with snow.

Adjusting his blue wool hat and pulling up the hood of his coat, he followed the other passengers down the stairs.

After clearing customs and immigration, Víctor retrieved his luggage and made his way to the lobby, scanning the crowd for the person who was supposed to meet him.

He had reserved a room at one of Stanley's hotels, and the hotel had promised to send someone to pick him up at the airport. In the lobby, he spotted a young man holding a sign with his name and the hotel's name on it.

"Good morning, I'm Víctor Cabot," he said as he approached.

"Good morning, sir. Welcome to the Falkland Islands. May I take your luggage? My name is Alejandro, and I'll be your driver."

"Thank you, Alejandro! *¿Hablás español?*" Víctor asked, noticing the man's name and accent.

"Yes, sir, I do. I'm Chilean… from Santiago. If you prefer, we can speak in Spanish."

"Yes, of course. I'm Uruguayan. Though, I could use the practice for my English."

"As you like, but you'll have no trouble here. There are many foreigners, and while English is the official language, Spanish is probably the second most commonly spoken. Please follow me; I've parked the vehicle in the lot."

Víctor immediately felt at ease. The people were friendly, and he quickly sensed a welcoming warmth.

"I'm already liking this place," Víctor said as they reached the parking lot and saw the cars driving on the left. "But I see you've got a very serious problem here."

"What do you mean?" Alejandro asked, looking a bit concerned.

"You're all driving on the wrong side of the road!"

Alejandro burst out laughing. "That's what I thought when I first got here," he replied. "But don't worry; you'll get used to the British system in no time. Maybe one accident or two at most," he joked.

The drive to the hotel took almost an hour, and during that time, Alejandro familiarized Víctor with some of the island's customs. He talked about the 1982 war, the wounds it left behind, the resilience it fostered among the islanders, and the economic benefits that had arisen indirectly—such as the United Kingdom granting more rights to the Falkland Islands to strengthen their autonomy. Alejandro also spoke about local jobs and industries. He shared that he had moved from Santiago only two years ago and felt very comfortable living there. He offered recommendations for tourist spots and tours departing from the hotel, though he warned that winter tours could be limited.

Víctor mostly listened. He didn't want to share the real reason for his visit to the Falkland Islands, preferring to pass as just another tourist. He simply mentioned that he was interested in writing a book about some of the island's stories and that he had spoken on the phone with Professor McIntyre, the museum director, whom he planned to visit after getting settled.

"Oh, you've already spoken with him? He's a very good person, deeply knowledgeable about the Falkland Islands and their history. I'm sure you'll find something interesting through him."

"Yes, I hope so," Víctor replied.

During the remainder of the drive, Víctor took in the rolling landscape and mountains. Some views reminded him of places in eastern Paysandú, with its hills and treeless fields, giving him a comforting sense of home.

He was surprised by the amount of traffic in such a sparsely populated area, home to fewer than 4,000 people. As Víctor gazed at the towering mountains along the winding road, where soldiers had once fought and died, an eerie chill ran down his spine. The land had witnessed war, and it still held its ghosts.

When they arrived in Stanley, Alejandro drove to the hotel on Ross Road, one of the city's main streets. The Malvina Hotel stood just across from the Falkland Islands Museum.

He parked in the back lot and helped Víctor carry his luggage to the reception desk. Before leaving, Alejandro handed Víctor his phone number. "If you need anything during your stay, just give me a call."

"Thank you, Alejandro. I appreciate it."

Check-in was quick, and by the time Víctor reached his room, it was already 4 p.m. The winter sun was beginning to fade. In these latitudes, daylight was scarce this time of year, so he decided to stay in, rest, and gather his thoughts.

His room opened onto a balcony overlooking the garden, with a beautiful view of Stanley Harbour's shimmering waters and the distant silhouette of rugged mountains. After a warm shower and unpacking, he settled at the desk to jot down a few ideas as the reality of finally being there began to sink in.

Later, with a steaming cup of coffee in hand, he gazed out the window. The lights of anchored ships swayed gently with the waves, their reflections flickering on the dark water. The town lay quiet, save for the whisper of the wind and the occasional passing vehicle.

A simple dinner at the hotel's restaurant ended his evening, and he turned in early, eager for the days ahead.

Chapter IX

Surprise

He woke up early in the morning, around five. He couldn't sleep anymore. Maybe it was the silence of the town, or the anxiety of not knowing what the following days would bring. And although it was Sunday, and he had nothing scheduled until eleven, he got out of bed.

He was sure he'd soon unravel the mysteries that had brought him there, but there were still too many unanswered questions, and that unsettled him.

He prepared his *mate*, arranged the armchair by the window, and sat down to enjoy his first sunrise in Stanley, watching the city wake up.

As daylight broke, despite the cold, he took advantage of the calm morning to go for a walk and familiarize himself with his surroundings. He also wanted to clear his mind, relax, and pass the time before meeting with the professor. He considered walking to the harbor to see where the *Fennia* might have been anchored, then heading to Port Louis that afternoon, depending on his discussion with the professor.

He still didn't know how to approach the owners of Port Louis to ask for permission to search their land at the site marked on Karl's map. What excuse could he use? Telling them he was looking for a treasure and the answer to Patrick's disappearance seemed far-fetched. They'd think he was crazy—though perhaps it was his only option.

He stepped outside to find that the snow on the ground had nearly disappeared, but the wind and biting cold were just as intense as the day before.

Víctor started walking along Ross Road, intending to cover its entire length to the far end of town. But as he passed the cemetery, something made him hesitate. On impulse, he changed course and stepped through the entrance.

The cemetery was the original burial ground of Port Stanley, nestled on a slope overlooking the bay. A cement wall and thick bushes framed its modest two-hectare expanse. He climbed the long staircase leading to the entrance, where a massive *Cross of Sacrifice* loomed—a solemn monument to those lost in the First and Second World Wars.

Inside, the air felt heavy with history. He wandered between the graves, reading names and dates etched into weathered stone. Some epitaphs spoke of love and loss, while others were mere markers of time.

Then, he stopped.

His breath caught as his gaze locked onto a name:

Annadee Bauer Fischer

For a moment, the world around him faded. He stared at the white marble slab, its smooth surface adorned with a cross and an inscription beneath her name:

To the living memory of
Annadee Bauer Fischer,
who departed this life on June 24, 1888,
at the age of 76.
Oh, dear mother, rest in peace.

But... if she was living in Montevideo, why is she here?

Confusion swelled inside him. He read the date again.

Yesterday was her anniversary.

A strange chill ran down his spine. *I arrived on the islands on the anniversary of her death.*

One hundred and twenty-nine years had passed.

He took a slow step back, his eyes drifting to the grave beside hers. Another tombstone bore the same surname:

Patricia Sans Bauer
1832–1923

Her daughter? Their daughter?

Fresh flowers rested at Annadee's grave, a quiet testament that someone still remembered her. The sight unsettled him. Standing there, surrounded by the silence of the past, he found himself trying to imagine what her life might have been like in this remote place during the 19th century.

How different everything must have been—no fast communication, no easy way to leave, dependent on sailing ships that could take weeks or months to reach civilization.

It must have been a hard and demanding life, he thought.

A sudden unease crept in. He checked his watch.

Damn. He had lost track of time. He needed to get back to the hotel immediately—his appointment with Professor McIntyre at the museum was at eleven sharp. With the building closed to the public, it would be the perfect setting for their conversation.

With one last glance at the grave, he turned and hurried down the path, the weight of history pressing against his thoughts.

By mid-morning, activity in Stanley had picked up noticeably. People he passed greeted him as if he were just another neighbor, which made him feel comfortable and at ease in these distant islands.

He went directly to the hotel to grab his laptop and notebook from his room. Then, crossing through the garden, he headed toward the Falkland Islands Museum. The museum complex was made up of several separate buildings with white walls and emerald-green corrugated metal roofs.

When he arrived, he knocked on the door, even though the parking lot was empty. Leaning toward the glass to peer inside, he found the interior deserted.

He probably won't take long to arrive, he thought.

To pass the time, he walked along the small pier that extended out into the bay. In his mind, he could almost picture the *Fennia* anchored there years ago.

Farther away, across the bay, the fishing boats he had seen the previous night continued to rock gently with the waves, waiting for their possible departure to sea. Behind them loomed Wireless Ridge, where one of the final battles of the 1982 war took place.

A green Land Rover drove into the parking lot and stopped in front of the museum doors. It was Professor McIntyre—he recognized him from the website photo. Víctor raised a hand in greeting from a distance and walked over to meet him.

"Professor, good morning," he said as he approached.

"Good morning. Mister Cabot, I presume? Welcome, welcome to the Falkland Islands and to my museum."

"Yes, thank you! How are you? It's a pleasure to finally meet you in person."

"Likewise," replied the professor as they shook hands. "How was your trip?"

"Very nice, although I always get nervous when I fly, but it was good, no mishaps."

The professor smiled and continued shaking his hand.

"I'm excited to learn what information you have about the disappearance of Patrick Sans McGowan."

Patrick's life was almost lost to the island's history, forgotten like many who were part of the early colonization of the Falklands. Yet, it remained an intriguing mystery due to the rumors of his treasure. The professor also wondered how someone from Uruguay had taken an interest in this story and why he would travel so far just to investigate a case that had been closed and forgotten for 186 years.

"I hope you're enjoying the Falkland Islands despite the wind and the cold. Quite different from your country, I imagine," he said.

"Yes, a little, but I really like it. It doesn't get this cold in Uruguay, but I lived in New York for many years, so I've experienced similar weather, although the wind here is something else."

"I would have advised you to come in the summer, but... I'm glad you're here now, Mr. Cabot."

"Please, call me Víctor."

"Okay, Víctor, and you can call me John. You know, I've been really excited to hear what you're writing and what you know about Patrick. How did you find out about him?"

"Well, I..."

"Actually, wait, Víctor. Let me unload these things from the Rover and open the museum. Then we'll chat in my office—it's more comfortable and warm there. Besides, I have some books and maps I want to show you."

Seeing John juggling several items, Víctor offered to help him.

"Well, now that you mention it, I have some artifacts in the back that you could help me unload."

"Sure, John, of course."

Víctor adjusted his backpack and headed to the back of the vehicle while John unlocked the tailgate.

"Ship lamps? Bronze? They look really old... and they smell awful," Víctor said as he examined them.

"Yes, Víctor, they do. They're probably from around the 1800s. They were pulled from the ocean yesterday by a fishing boat's nets, north of here. We'll clean and restore them. After that, I'll investigate which shipwreck they might be from. There are many in that area."

Víctor picked up one lamp while the professor carried the other, then John closed the tailgate and led him inside the building.

Once inside, they set the lamps on the floor and walked toward the office at the back of the same building.

When they arrived, Víctor was struck by the number of photographs adorning the walls. Some were old, others more recent, and many depicted scenes from the 1982 war between Argentina and the United Kingdom.

"Take a seat, Víctor. I'll give you a tour later. Would you like some coffee or tea?"

"Yes, please. Coffee would be great. Thank you."

Víctor sat down on one of the red leather sofas but soon stood up again to take a closer look at the photos on another wall.

"Your museum is fascinating, Professor. How long have you been the director?"

"Since 2015. Just two years so far. We've been in these buildings since 2014. We've grown quickly because things keep turning up—lost artifacts, both old and new.

There are several people on the board, and I'll introduce you to the rest later. In winter, we're closed on Sundays."

"Then I must apologize, Professor, for making you work today."

"Not at all," John said with a smile. "I had to come anyway to drop off those lamps. I didn't want them sitting in my Rover all day. With all the encrustations on them, they were starting to smell bad. Besides, to be honest, I wanted to meet you as soon as possible—I'm very curious about your part of the story and how you came to learn about Patrick Sans McGowan."

John handed Víctor a cup of coffee.

"Here you go. Sugar? Cream?"

"No, this is perfect, thanks, John. I see you have a lot of photos from the war here in your office. Did you participate in 1982?"

"No, not directly. But I lived here, so I experienced it. That's another story altogether—it left deep scars on this place, on everyone. Very different from what happened with Patrick. That war won't be forgotten, unlike his life. So tell me, how did you come to learn about this case? You mentioned documents in Montevideo. Do you have them with you?"

"No, I don't. I didn't think they'd be useful for the research here, but you can find everything online."

"Great. If you tell me the site, I'll look it up later."

"It took me quite a while to find that information, believe me. I spent hours at the computer."

Without knowing what was truly at stake or what consequences there could be, Víctor preferred not to share more than he had to. He wouldn't mention the box and its contents, or Hans and Karl, or even the

Fennia. First, he needed to understand what it was all about. Until he knew more, he wouldn't reveal anything—not even to Juan Ramírez, who had no idea about his discoveries.

"It was actually pure coincidence, John," Víctor said, leaning forward. "I was helping a friend with something totally unrelated—another case. But as I followed one lead after another, I came across an old document mentioning Patrick and his disappearance. That stuck with me. The more I read, the more I wanted to know. Then I called the police in the islands, and when you told me the case was still open, I knew I had to come."

John studied him for a moment. "So, just like that, you dropped everything to investigate and write about him?"

"Well… yes. Why not? The story intrigued me. Besides, I do freelance work for several newspapers as a photographer and journalist. What I've found so far has only deepened my curiosity. Once my investigation is complete, I'll share all the details with you, Professor. I have a strong feeling about this case."

"Ah, I see. And please, just call me John."

"Okay, that's fine… John."

"You'll have your work cut out for you here, then. I've tried myself to find out what happened and kept hitting dead ends. I didn't know about that document online, though. It must have been uploaded recently. Still, I'm not sure how much it will help us solve the mystery, my friend, but if you like investigating, you'll find a lot of fascinating things here. At the very least, you'll have enough material to craft a good story. Personally, I don't think this can ever be solved anymore. Too much time has passed, and there's nowhere left to look."

"Well, you don't have much faith in me, Professor," Víctor said, smiling.

"Sorry… I didn't mean to underestimate your abilities," John replied, embarrassed. "It's just… it's just how I see things. I've lost hope of ever finding out where he went."

Víctor took a sip of his coffee to avoid saying too much and then asked,

"Would it be possible for me to borrow those books and maps you mentioned for further study?"

"I'm afraid not," John replied. "These books and maps are very old, as you might imagine, and it's museum policy. However, we're open every day during the week. You can come in any time during our hours. No problem."

"Alright, thank you very much, John. I want to let you know that once I finish my investigation, and if—thanks to your help and a bit of luck—I uncover what happened, I'll provide you with a detailed report. That way, you can include it with your research. Oh, and before I forget, I wanted to ask you about a grave. This morning, while I was exploring Stanley, I passed through the cemetery and found the grave of Annadee Bauer Fischer. She was the one who filed the report about Patrick's disappearance in Montevideo shortly after her arrival there. According to the report, she seemed to indicate that Montevideo was her new residence. How is it that her grave is here? Obviously, she returned at some point, but what happened? When did she come back? Do you know anything?"

"Oh, yes. And of course I really hope you can figure out what happened. I would love to read your report once you finish. As for Annadee's grave? Yes, she was a very influential figure in Stanley's early days. Records show that she first came to the islands with her parents in 1829, but they returned to Montevideo in early 1832, shortly after the *USS Lexington* attacked Port Louis. Much later, she decided to return to the Falkland Islands in 1847 and lived here until her death. She brought her daughter, Patricia, with her, who was fifteen years old at the time. Apparently, Patricia was Patrick's daughter. It's said that Annadee came back looking for him, but she never found him or learned anything more about his fate."

"Fifteen years is a long time. A lot could have happened during that period," Víctor noted.

"Yes, it is. But it seems Annadee never gave up hope all those years. She clearly never forgot him. He was her first and only love," John said, leaning back in his chair. "And tell me, what else have you discovered in your investigation?"

Not wanting to reveal everything he knew, Víctor simply said,

"Well, not much more. Apart from her report, I haven't been able to find anything else about her family in Uruguay. That's why I'm here. I figured the best way to complete this story was to visit the places where Patrick and Annadee were."

"That seems like a good idea, though I don't think there's much left that could help us uncover the truth. There are no witnesses left—that's for certain," John said, getting up to refill his coffee and offering some to Víctor.

"No, thanks, John. I've had enough coffee for now. Could you show me those books and maps? I'd like to have a look."

"Of course, Víctor."

John set his cup down on the sideboard and motioned for Víctor to follow him.

As they were leaving the office, the phone rang. John excused himself, saying it was probably his wife, as she was the only one who knew he would be there, and went to answer.

"Hello? Yes, darling, I'm with him... Okay, hang on a moment, let me sort something out here, and I'll call you back in five minutes, alright? ... Bye ... I love you too."

"Yes, it was her. Come on, I'll take you to the study room so you can start looking through the documents. Follow me, please."

They walked down a long, narrow hallway toward a staircase that led to the second floor, where the study room was located. The professor pulled several map tubes and books from a cabinet and placed them on the large oak table in the center of a well-lit room, its big windows offering a sweeping view of the bay.

"Here you go, Víctor. I'll leave these with you. The books already have pages marked that might interest you. I marked them myself back when I was investigating this case. And as for the maps, well, you'll see their relevance when you look at them. This should keep you busy for a while. I'll leave you alone while I make a call to my wife and take care of a few things. I'll check on you as soon as I'm done."

"Alright, perfect. Thank you, John."

The professor closed the door, leaving Víctor alone in the study room. He knew he wouldn't have much time to go through all those books, so he decided to focus on the maps first. He removed them from their tubes and laid them out on the table. One was a map of East Falkland, also known as *Isla Soledad*. Another depicted the northern part of the island, known as the San Luis Peninsula, where the old capital was located. The smallest map was an old plan of Port Louis, back when it was the capital of the Falkland Islands and under French control.

The settlement was larger than Víctor had expected. The map detailed all the houses and buildings from that time, along with the names of their owners, the people who lived there, or the purposes for which the structures were used. It also marked other important sites in the town.

Víctor took out his phone and snapped several photos of all the maps so he could later compare them, back at the hotel, with the one Karl Henning had. Doing so now carried the risk of John returning, seeing it, and prompting questions. It wasn't the right time for that yet.

With all this new information, Víctor felt he was getting very close to solving the mystery. He was confident he had found the missing link in the story. Now, with these scaled maps and measurements, it would be much easier to calculate distances and pinpoint the site.

Just as he was jotting down notes in his notebook, Professor McIntyre returned to the room.

"My dear Víctor, I'm so sorry to have left you alone. My wife is organizing a gathering with friends and family tonight, and she needed me to pick up a few things from the supermarket. By the way, you're invited."

"Oh, no, no! Thank you so much, but I really wouldn't want to impose—especially after you've already gone out of your way to come here on a Sunday."

"Please, it's no imposition. It would be a pleasure to have a Uruguayan in our home. When we found out you were coming this weekend, it was too late to cancel anything. Everything was already organized, so we just decided to set an extra plate at the table. I understand you might be tired, but the invitation still stands."

"Well, thank you. Yes, traveling is exhausting. And don't forget, I only have a week to investigate, write, and photograph everything I need."

"Yes, of course. But we'd be delighted to host you in our home. Besides, there's a young woman, a friend of my wife, who's also from your country. She might have some insights that could help with your story. I think you'd really enjoy it."

With John's persistence, Víctor reconsidered the invitation. Maybe he was right. Plus, he knew he wouldn't have another chance to meet the islanders in such an intimate setting.

"Alright, John, you've convinced me. I'll come to your house tonight."

"Perfect! Excellent decision!" John said, clapping his hands cheerfully. "The official invitation is at five in the afternoon, and dinner will be served about an hour later. We might even get to continue our discussion then. For now, though, I'm afraid I have to leave before my wife gets more nervous."

"Oh, yes, of course. I understand. No problem—I was thinking of inviting you to lunch at the hotel, but I see you won't be able to."

"You're right, Víctor, not today at least. But there will be another opportunity."

"I really enjoyed looking at the maps and plans, John. I took photos of them. I'll study the books tomorrow when I come back."

"Perfect. You'll be more rested and focused by then."

"Yes, I hope so."

"Alright, let's head out. Do you need a ride somewhere in Stanley? To a restaurant perhaps?"

"Thanks, John, don't worry about it. I'll just head to the hotel, grab a bite there, and get some writing done."

They left the museum a little past noon, and John assured him he'd be back to pick him up at five sharp.

Víctor waved goodbye, crossed the street to the hotel, and went straight to his room. As soon as he shut the door behind him, he pulled out his phone and Karl's copy of the map.

After studying them closely, there was no doubt—they pointed to the same place: Port Louis.

Yes, yes! he muttered under his breath. *Got it.*

Chapter X

Dinner with the McIntyres

It was nearing five in the afternoon when Víctor went down to the lobby to wait for Professor McIntyre. The sun had just dipped below the horizon, and darkness was beginning to settle. A strong northwesterly wind, relentless and biting, made him wonder if he would ever get used to it.

Knowing the English reputation for punctuality, Víctor assumed he wouldn't be waiting long. So, at exactly 5:00 pm, when he spotted a green Land Rover pulling up to the Ross Road esplanade, he stepped outside without waiting for John to come in and fetch him. The cold wind urged him to quicken his pace and get into the vehicle.

"Good evening, Professor— " he began as he slid into the passenger seat—only to stop abruptly when he realized the driver wasn't John McIntyre. "Oh… sorry. I think I got into the wrong car. You're not John."

Embarrassed, Víctor quickly scrambled out, standing beside the vehicle, feeling awkward and confused.

The driver, a young woman, rolled down the window with a soft smile. "No, no, you're not mistaken!"

Víctor raised an eyebrow. "Well, young lady, you don't look much like John McIntyre, so I don't think I'm the one who's wrong here."

She chuckled. "Very funny. But... you're Víctor Cabot, right? From Uruguay?"

"Yes," he answered, surprised. "And I'm waiting for Professor McIntyre. This vehicle looks just like his, which is why I got confused."

She nodded.

"You're correct about that. It's identical, but not the same. Maybe you haven't noticed yet, but these are quite popular here. I'm Diana Díaz. John asked me to pick you up. Didn't he mention there was a Uruguayan guest?"

"Well, yes, he did... but he didn't say you'd be the one picking me up."

"Oh, I'm sorry, Víctor. He couldn't come. He called me earlier and asked if I could pick you up because he was running behind schedule and wouldn't make it on time. He had to help his wife with a few things."

"Ah, now I understand," Víctor said. "So, may I hop in?"

"Of course, go ahead. I won't bite," she said playfully.

Víctor got in the car again and shook her hand.

"Nice to meet you... Diana, right? So, you're Uruguayan too?"

"That's right. From Mercedes, Soriano. And you?"

"Paysandú."

"Ah! We're both from the interior," she said warmly as she started the engine and pulled onto the road. "So, is this your first time here?"

"Yes, my first. It looks like a beautiful place, though the wind is a bit of a nuisance, isn't it?"

"Yeah, it is. It takes time to get used to. What do you think of Stanley?"

"I like it a lot. It reminds me of a place I lived in, out east on Long Island, New York, though this is a bit more colorful. It's very charming and neat. I like it."

"I'm glad to hear that."

"And you? Have you lived here long?"

"About two years."

"Oh, not very long. Are you fully settled in?"

"You could say so. Anyway, tell me, what brought you to the Falklands? Did you come for a vacation, work, or maybe to live?"

"Well, a little bit of everything. And I may even move here—why not? Didn't John tell you anything?"

"No. Actually, I'm more of a friend of his wife, Elizabeth. We worked together at the school until she retired. I'm a Spanish teacher at the secondary school."

"Oh, how interesting! I didn't know that. Well, I'm here investigating a missing person case. I'm writing a story about it for a newspaper. A thread in my investigation led me here."

"A missing person? From the 1982 war, perhaps? An Argentine?"

"No, not from that war. This goes way back—1832. A man named Patrick Sans McGowan. Have you heard of him?"

"Yes, several times. John knows quite a bit about him. I suppose you've discussed it with him."

"Yes, that's why I reached out to him. He told me he'd done some research, but they never found out what happened."

"And if you don't mind me asking, why are you writing about this particular case? I mean, it may be a little boring, don't you think?"

"It's a long story, and you may be right, but I find it intriguing. While I was investigating another case, I found information about this one. Patrick's fiancée, Annadee Bauer Fischer, lived here in the Falklands for a few years. Later, when she moved back to Montevideo, she filed a report about his disappearance. Apparently, they were supposed to board a ship together, but he vanished before they could."

"Annadee Bauer Fischer? There's a grave here with that name. Is it the same person?"

"Yes, according to the professor, she returned here years later."

"Aha! I know the family—well, their descendants, I mean. They live on a farm north of here, about a 45-minute drive from Stanley, in Isthmus Camp."

"Wait, what, really? Are you serious? That's incredible! I had no idea. The professor didn't mention that."

She rolled her eyes with a slight smile. "Ah, that professor... always so forgetful!" It must have slipped his mind. I believe he's spoken with them before."

"I'd love to meet them! What are their names? How can I get in touch with the family?" Víctor asked, his excitement evident.

Diana stopped the car and said, "I'll tell you later. Right now, it's best if we go inside. We've arrived, and they must be waiting for us." Then she opened her door.

"Oh, this is it? That wasn't very far."

Diana smiled and tilted her head. "Nothing is far in Stanley, Víctor. Let's go!"

Víctor let Diana lead the way, following her across the large garden that surrounded the house, bordered by white picket fences. They walked along a cobblestone path to the entrance, where Diana knocked on the door. Almost immediately, John opened it.

"Hello, Diana! How are you? And you brought your fellow countryman—thank you! Welcome to my home!" He patted Víctor on the back with a warm smile. "Come in, please. Make yourself at home."

They removed their coats, and John hung them on the coat rack before leading them into the living room. The cozy space, warmed by a fireplace, featured large windows that overlooked the bay. Though adorned with delicate white lace curtains, the windows still offered a stunning view of the bay.

Standing at the doorway, John quieted the room and announced, "Dear friends and family, I'd like to introduce Mr. Víctor Cabot, a new friend of the family. This is his first visit to the Falkland Islands."

Several people greeted him warmly from their seats, some raising their glasses in a toast, offering simple greetings—"Hello," "Welcome,"

"Bienvenido." Víctor raised his hand in response, acknowledging their hospitality.

Nearby guests shook his hand and introduced themselves, their warmth making him feel instantly at ease. The camaraderie of the islanders reminded him of home, their kindness genuine and inviting.

After a while, John introduced him to his wife, Elizabeth. They chatted in the kitchen as she prepared refreshments before returning to the living room to join the others.

Víctor considered pulling John aside for a private conversation, hoping to gather more information for his investigation. But as he looked around the lively room, filled with laughter and the clinking of glasses, he knew it wouldn't be possible that evening. Instead, he allowed himself to settle into the gathering. He listened, observed, and soaked in the atmosphere, knowing that sometimes, the best clues came from casual conversations rather than direct inquiries.

After some time, Víctor spotted Diana among the guests and resumed their earlier conversation from the car ride.

"Ah, there you are! The people here are amazing. Are they always this friendly?"

Diana nodded. "Yes, they're very kind."

"I love their energy. It really puts me at ease."

"It was the same for me when I first came here. It's one of the reasons I decided to stay."

Víctor shifted the conversation back to what had been on his mind. "I've been thinking about what you said earlier. You mentioned knowing Annadee Bauer's relatives. How can I reach them? Do they live in Stanley, or are they always out at that place you mentioned?"

"Well, her daughter, Ashley, works with me at the secondary school. But she left yesterday with her daughter to visit her parents for the holidays. She won't be back until the weekend after next."

"Ah, just my luck. I'm heading back to Uruguay next Sunday."

"They live nearby, though. I've been to their farm a couple of times with Ashley. It's on the road to Port Louis."

"Really? I was planning to head to that area anyway."

"Then it might work out. Maybe you could visit their farm."

"That's a great idea. Do you think they'd be open to talking about Annadee with a journalist, or are they more private?"

"I'm not sure. I haven't talked much about it with her, but I can give her a call tomorrow and ask. It's no trouble."

"Oh, yes, please. Would you do that for me?"

"Of course."

"Thank you so much. Just let her know it's for an article in a Uruguayan newspaper."

"Absolutely, no problem," Diana reassured him.

Elizabeth and John went to the dining table in the adjacent room. Tapping a glass like a small bell, they called everyone to take their seats. The guests approached as Elizabeth guided them to their places. She seated Diana and Víctor together, directly across from her.

Once everyone was seated, John stood up and said:

"I'd like to thank all of you for coming to our home tonight. Friendship and good manners between brothers and friends are very important. We welcome everyone, and today, especially, our new friend Víctor, who has come from so far away. Elizabeth and I wish him success in his project, and to everyone here, a long and prosperous life!" He then raised his glass and made a toast with the group.

"And now, let's eat—I'm starving!"

During dinner, one of the guests, whom Víctor had not yet had the chance to speak with, asked him what part of Uruguay he was from.

"I'm from Paysandú. Have you ever been there, you know where it is?"

"No, I haven't, but I used to be a sailor before moving here. I've been to Montevideo and Nueva Palmira on cargo ships but never made it that far upriver. I've heard of it many times. It's farther up the Uruguay River, right?"

"That's correct," Víctor replied.

"Wasn't that where the *Fennia* ended up?" another guest chimed in.

Víctor was startled to hear the name.

"The *Fennia*?" he asked, trying to sound casual.

The guest, who appeared to be at least twice Víctor's age and seemed well-versed in ships and their histories, nodded.

"Yes, the *Fennia* was an old cargo ship. It was anchored here in the bay for years. Remember it?" he asked the others. "The one that lost its masts and was brought here for repairs that never happened. Later, the

Falkland Islands Company bought it to store wool and other goods. It was eventually sold to be turned into a museum, but somehow it ended up abandoned and dismantled in your city. That was a long time ago, though. Not many people remember it anymore," he said.

"And how do you remember?" Víctor asked.

"Ah, because of my uncle... He worked as a guard when it was used as a prison. He always told us stories about that ship. Did you know it housed German prisoners at the start of World War II?"

"No, I didn't know that," Víctor lied.

"Yes, it was. Later, most of them were transferred to South Africa. Well, almost all of them."

"That's a fascinating story. But why do you say 'almost all of them'? What do you mean?" Víctor asked.

"Well... a few days before the ship that was supposed to take them sailed, two of the prisoners escaped. They jumped into the bay from the *Fennia* at night, or so it was said. They vanished and were never seen again. Not alive or dead. But the whole matter was more or less hushed up. We only learned about it at home because my uncle told the story years later, after the war ended."

"Interesting," Víctor added. "And who were they? Do you remember their names?"

"Oh, no, I can't recall that much. It was a long time ago. I only know they were the two sailors captured here on the islands. Apparently, they were survivors from a warship sunk near the coast. But why are you asking about their names? They were probably damned Nazis. Yes, that's what they were," the man concluded, visibly irritated.

"Are you planning another story, Mr. Cabot?" John asked.

"Well, maybe. It's my journalist spirit—always asking questions," Víctor replied with a smile.

However, Víctor knew the reason for his curiosity. It was obvious to him that those two prisoners had been Karl Henning and Hans Schneider. Obviously.

"I might have something about that ship in the museum. I'll look for it tomorrow and show it to you," John said. "Now, what a coincidence," he added thoughtfully, "that the *Fennia* ended up over there and you, being from there, ended up here."

"Yes, that's true," Víctor said. Then, making air quotes, he added, "I just hope I don't end up 'dismantled' here."

Everyone burst into laughter.

Elizabeth, with a mischievous smile, looked at Víctor and then at Diana. Pointing at them, she said:

"Yes, and I hope the two of you don't end up stuck here… together."

The laughter grew even louder. Víctor and Diana felt their cheeks flush but said nothing, avoiding eye contact as they tried to downplay the remark.

After that, Víctor became thoughtful. *What could have happened to them? Did they manage to survive? And if they did, where did they go? After all, they were on an island*, he questioned silently.

He didn't think it was appropriate to ask any more questions at the moment, not wanting to raise suspicions or invite questions he preferred not to answer.

When dinner ended, some guests decided to leave, explaining that they had to wake up early the next day, while others stayed a bit longer.

"Would anyone like tea or coffee? It's freshly made. If you'd like some, head over to the kitchen."

Víctor went to fetch a cup and asked Diana if she wanted one as well.

"Yes, how kind of you," she replied.

"Not at all. Now, excuse me, you're taking me back to the hotel, right?"

"Of course, I live a bit beyond the hotel, almost at the edge of town. It's on the way."

"Perfect. So whenever you're ready to leave, we'll go."

"Okay. Should we have the coffee first?"

"Yes, of course."

A little while later, when the other guests began saying their goodbyes, Diana and Víctor decided to leave as well, not wanting to be the last ones.

"John, it's been a real pleasure sharing this dinner with both of you, your family, and friends," Víctor said. "Thank you so much for having me. I've learned a lot about your customs and a bit of your history too. Elizabeth, everything was delicious. Thank you again."

"You're welcome, and thank you for coming. I'm sure we'll see each other again before you leave. I hope your story is a success and that you can find all the information you need to write it," Elizabeth said warmly.

"Thank you. With your husband's help, I'm sure I will."

"Thank you, Víctor. I'll see you tomorrow at the museum then? Come by whenever you like—I'll be there all day," John added. Then he turned to Diana, thanking her for coming and bringing Víctor.

"Of course. It was a pleasure. See you soon; everything was wonderful."

The night was freezing—far colder than when they had arrived. Víctor looked up, marveling at the sky scattered with countless stars, more than he had seen in years. Leaning against the Land Rover's hood, he gazed at the vast expanse above him. He cupped his hands around his mouth, breathing warm air into them, the misty vapor a reminder of the biting cold.

"You can see the stars so clearly here," he murmured. "It's incredible. I can't remember the last time I saw a sky like this."

"Yeah, isn't it amazing?" Diana stepped beside him, tilting her head back. "There's barely any light pollution here. It's beautiful, right?"

She paused, then asked softly, "What do you think when you see all this? I mean… what's out there? Where does it all end?"

Víctor sighed, lost in thought. After a brief silence, he said, "Just… infinity. Us and infinity. And I don't think the universe has an end… or a beginning, for that matter."

"Really?" she asked, surprised. "You don't believe there was a beginning? Or maybe… a creation?"

Víctor shook his head. "No, not at all. Everything we've discovered so far makes me think it's always been here. It wasn't made, wasn't created. It just exists."

Diana's gaze remained on the stars. "Well, that's an interesting concept," she murmured.

"It's more than a concept to me," Víctor said, his voice steady. "It feels like a fact. The idea of a beginning or an end—at least as we understand them—doesn't make sense to me. The universe just... is. Always transforming, always evolving, with endless cycles of big bangs and rebirths, but without a true start or finish. Can something really come from nothing? Like magic? I don't think so. For something to exist, something must have existed before. So, to me, the answer's obvious." He shrugged, offering a faint smile. "But... who knows? Anything's possible."

Diana turned to him. "So then, what is the true purpose of our existence?"

"I think purpose is something we define for ourselves, rather than something given to us."

Víctor quickly changed the subject and asked about her friend, Ashley.

"You're so impatient. I already told you I'll call her tomorrow, and once I know something, I'll let you know. Give me your number so I can ring you up."

"I'll give it to you, but I don't have service here. You can call me at the hotel."

"Alright, consider it done. Now let's go—I'm freezing."

It wasn't very late, but the streets of Stanley were deserted.

"It's so peaceful," Víctor said as they drove through town.

"Yes. The bars and restaurants close at 11pm, especially in winter. There's not much nightlife this time of year," Diana explained. After a brief pause, she added, "By the way, I don't know if I mentioned it, but we're on vacation this week. If you need help, I could take you to my friend's farm if you like. It's been a while since I last went there, and it'd be a good excuse."

"Thanks, but... I think that's asking too much."

"Not at all, quite the opposite. Though I heard you're going to the museum tomorrow, right? So maybe we can plan the farm trip for Tuesday or Wednesday. What do you think? I'll check with her to see if she's available to have us over."

"Yes, tomorrow I'll be doing some research at the museum. Planning it by then sounds better."

Diana parked in front of the hotel but didn't turn off the engine.

"It was nice meeting you, Víctor."

"Same here, Diana. Thanks for everything," he said, extending his hand to shake hers. But she clasped it, pulling him closer to give him a kiss on the cheek.

"Let's say goodbye the Uruguayan way, shall we?"

"Of course, Diana. Why not?"

Víctor got out and shut the door. Before leaving, Diana rolled down the window and said, "If you have some free time tomorrow, I could show you around Stanley and the surrounding areas. Do you have a camera? We could take some photos. What do you think?"

"Absolutely!" he replied instinctively. "That's a great idea!"

"I'll call you tomorrow," she said with a smile, winking her left eye playfully before driving off.

He stood there for a while, watching her Rover disappear down the road into the night, until the silence and solitude returned.

The hotel lobby was empty, except for the concierge, who was quietly watching TV when Víctor entered.

"Good evening, Mr. Cabot."

"Good and cold," he replied, rubbing his hands together as he made his way to his room.

He had intended to write about the evening's events, but it was already late.

Tomorrow will be another day, he thought.

Chapter XI

Visit to the Museum and Surroundings

When he woke up, the pounding headache reminded him he had had too many beers the night before. He squinted at the dim light filtering through the curtains and turned toward the window. The sun hadn't risen yet. Over the bay, the waning moon cast flickering silver streaks on the restless water. Without lifting his head from the pillow, he glanced at the clock on the nightstand—nearly six. He lingered there a moment, the echoes of laughter and conversation drifting back to him, along with the memory of Diana.

Not wanting to let the details slip away, he forced himself up. A quick shower helped clear the fog in his mind as he pieced together the night. Then, with a steaming *mate* in hand, he sat down to write.

Diana's image surfaced—the warmth of her smile, the playful wink as she said goodbye. She was charming, undeniably so. But Víctor quickly reminded himself of the inevitable. By Sunday, he'd be gone, and she would be nothing more than a fleeting memory. No point in letting his mind wander down a path that led nowhere. He exhaled sharply, shaking his head, only to regret it as pain throbbed in his temples.

Relax, Víctor. You've got everything under control, he muttered.

The cursor blinked on the blank page, taunting him. For a long moment, he stared at it, his thoughts refusing to settle. But as soon as his fingers began moving across the keyboard, the words flowed, pushing aside Diana and all the distractions he didn't want to entertain.

Then he recalled the conversation with the older man during dinner—the one who said his uncle had been a guard aboard the *Fennia*.

Well, that's another mystery solved, he thought.

Now Víctor understood why the box had been left on the *Fennia* and why no one had retrieved it. Hans and Karl's escape was undoubtedly a snap decision, leaving no time for anything else.

Perhaps there had been a mutiny, threats, or issues with the other prisoners. Maybe the plan to escape was rushed and improvised. Who knows? But something had happened to make them leave without the map, Víctor thought.

In any case, the puzzle was beginning to take shape.

After finishing his notes, he closed his laptop and put it away. He wouldn't write any more that morning.

He finished his *mate* fifteen minutes before nine, packed his belongings into his backpack, bundled up, and headed to the museum.

By the time he arrived, it was already open, and several people were browsing through the rooms filled with artifacts, photographs, and relics. They appeared to be tourists from a cruise ship that had docked the night before.

When he checked in at reception, he was told the professor was in the workshop, and they pointed to one of the adjacent warehouses visible through the window. Víctor made his way there.

He entered unnoticed by John and his assistant, who were engrossed in their work. The warehouse was filled with antiques, pieces of ships of all kinds, paintings, and artwork, giving it a mysterious and fascinating atmosphere.

"Good morning!"

The two men looked up from behind the lanterns that Víctor and John had retrieved the previous day and were now restoring. Adjusting his glasses with a finger, John replied:

"Good morning, Víctor. How are you? I was expecting you... and working. These lanterns have so many barnacles and grime stuck to them. You can tell how long they've been underwater. Anyway, let me introduce you to Ethan, a collaborator at the museum. Ethan, this is Víctor, from Uruguay. He's visiting and researching an article for his newspaper."

John then walked into an adjoining room, motioning for Víctor to follow.

"Before we head to the main room," he said, "I have something you might find interesting—a box of items from *Fennia*. It's one of our pending projects. I had forgotten about it, but after you left yesterday, I remembered I had several things from that ship. If you're interested, you can go through it and see if anything is useful to you."

"Really? Absolutely, I'm interested."

"Great. Come on, it's over here."

Víctor had no idea what he might find, but it was worth seeing what had been retrieved from the *Fennia* before it left Port Stanley. There could be more clues about Hans and Karl that no one had noticed.

"You can take anything you want to the main room if you'd like to study it more closely, but don't mix it with the other collections."

"Of course, no problem."

As they walked through a storage area cluttered with objects awaiting restoration, the professor stopped in front of an enormous green trunk reinforced with metal and leather straps—the kind once used for travel. Nearby, other boxes overflowed with artifacts, maps, old books, and various papers.

Professor McIntyre opened the trunk and left it open, inviting Víctor to explore its contents.

Almost immediately, something caught Víctor's attention. Inside the trunk, resting on one of the shelves, was a wooden box that looked strikingly similar to the one Juan Ramirez had given him. Víctor froze, deep in thought. Could it be possible that this box also had a hidden compartment like the other one? Might something be concealed within it?

The professor's voice pulled him out of his reverie.

"Are you all right, Víctor? You look like you've seen a ghost."

"Yes, I'm fine. I was just thinking about *Fennia.*"

"Ah, of course. Well, I'll leave you to it. Call me when you're ready to head to the main room."

"All right, will do."

John turned and left.

The first thing Víctor did was take the box and open it. It was empty, but identical to the other one, albeit in better condition. Its white-and-blue label with the manufacturer's mark was still well-preserved, and the wood and locks looked almost new. He tried to remove the interior molding to see if something might also be hidden inside, but it wouldn't budge. Regardless, he decided to take it with him to examine later in the study room.

Next, he investigated the other items from the *Fennia*. His primary interest was in finding papers, letters, objects from World War II, or anything from the era when the ship served as a prison for the Germans. He hoped to uncover more information about Hans and Karl.

Sifting through the artifacts, he found a folder containing receipts and various documents from that time, along with additional letters written by prisoners in German. He quickly skimmed through them, looking for any familiar names, but found none. Still, he decided to take them along to translate later, in case they held important clues.

Once he finished going through everything, he placed the items of interest in a box and went to find John.

"All done, Víctor? Need anything else?" John asked when he saw him.

"No, I think this will keep me busy for quite a while."

They said goodbye to Ethan and headed to the study room where the other maps and books were kept.

Once there, John explained a bit more about what he had discovered regarding Patrick. He also handed Víctor another book that contained information about the *Fennia*.

"All right, I'll leave you to your research now," John said. "If there's anything you don't understand, we can go over it later if you like. And if you'd like some coffee or tea, feel free to stop by my office. No problem at all."

"Thank you, John. That's very kind of you. I'll probably have plenty of questions later on."

John waved and left, closing the door behind him.

"Now, let's get to work!" Víctor said to himself.

He placed his backpack on the table, took out his laptop, notebook, and pencils, and set his camera off to the side. Then he sat down, grabbed one of the oldest books, and began flipping through its marked pages.

Most of the stories in those books were ones he had already read online during his research in Uruguay. While they included a few more details, the essence remained the same. One book that caught his interest told the stories of various individuals who had lived in Port Louis during its early days: Antonio *"El Gaucho"* or *"Antook"* Rivero and his murder on March 26, 1833; Antonina Roxa, who died in 1869 and was buried in Stanley Cemetery; Luis Vernet, Pedro Varela, and others. These figures were contemporaries of Annadee and Patrick.

What stood out to him was the lack of anything related to the *Fennia* in the professor's research on the disappearances. This suggested that John was unaware of the connection between that ship and Karl, Hans, or Patrick and Annadee.

Still, Víctor had yet to figure out how Karl learned about the *Liberty Rose* and Patrick, and why he had written those names on the sketch. He also didn't know if Hans and Karl had survived their escape, and if they did, where they might have gone.

Finding nothing about the *Liberty Rose* and wondering why information about that ship was missing, he decided to head to John's office.

He found the professor at his desk, typing away on his computer.

"Hey!" Víctor called, but John didn't respond. He seemed so engrossed in his work that he didn't hear him.

Víctor went straight to the coffee maker and, as he poured himself a cup, he asked:

"Do you think someone could survive jumping into the bay from a ship?"

John stopped typing, removed his glasses, and looked up.

"What do you mean?" John asked, raising an eyebrow.

"Do you remember the conversation with your friends last night? They talked about an escape from *Fennia*."

"Ah, you're talking about the prisoners? Well, yes and no. It depends on a lot of things. Did they have a boat waiting for them? Did they swim to the other shore? Were they thrown overboard, or were they perhaps "disappeared"? I think we'll never know, because, as my friend Murdoch said last night, they kept things hidden. It's like the ones who escaped from

Alcatraz in San Francisco—remember? No one ever found out what happened to them," he replied, turning back to his computer.

"Yeah, maybe you're right," Víctor said, then quickly asked, "And what about the *Liberty Rose*? Do you know anything? Why is there so little information?"

"Do you remember the bronze lamps?" the professor asked.

"Yes, but you didn't answer my question," Víctor insisted.

The professor lifted his eyes from the computer, looked him in the eye, and repeated, "Do you remember the bronze lamps? They're from the *Liberty Rose*. Incredible, isn't it? We just finished cleaning them, and we found the ship's name engraved on them."

"Wait... what? The ones we took out of your Rover yesterday? The ones you were working on with Ethan?" Víctor asked in disbelief.

"Yes, those exactly. We found the name *Liberty Rose* engraved at the base."

Víctor nearly dropped his cup, unable to believe it... or the coincidence.

"Are you sure?" he asked, almost speechless.

"Yes. Now we have proof that it existed. I'm checking the London records to see if there's any additional information," John replied, returning to his computer.

"Did you know it was said that Patrick had found a wrecked ship with that name on the coast?"

"Yes, of course, but they were just rumors. This changes things now," John said.

Víctor took a sip of his coffee, placed the cup on the desk, and sank into the couch, reflecting on all the coincidences that had led him to this moment. He could have ignored the call from the newspaper's editor, declined the job to photograph the fishing boats, or never noticed the remains of the *Fennia* on the riverbank. The box with the map could have gone undiscovered, misplaced, or never mentioned by Ramirez, and he himself might not have found the hidden map. He arrived in the Falkland Islands on the anniversary of Annadee's passing, and on the same day, they found the *Liberty Rose's* lamps.

If destiny wasn't prewritten, then somehow, he was helping to write it. Though… was that a good or bad thing? he wondered.

The professor glanced over the top of his screen and said,

"I'll keep looking into that ship. If there's no record, I think we might be talking about a vessel built somewhere that didn't keep logs or maybe a ship that was captured, turned to piracy, and had its name changed."

"That's possible, John," Víctor said. "This is all very interesting. Where were the lamps found?"

"I don't have the coordinates with me right now. The captain of the fishing boat gave them to me, but I can't recall where I left that note. It must be in the Rover, but I do know it was east of Berkeley Sound, near Volunteer Point. There are many wrecked ships out there. The story about Patrick finding a ship named that couldn't be confirmed… until now. This changes history."

"Yes, it seems that way. This is fascinating," Víctor said, leaving the professor immersed in his computer once again.

Back in the study room, Víctor sat down to review his notes and maps, trying to draw some final conclusions. The discovery of the *Liberty Rose* could either help or hinder his investigation. He wasn't sure which just yet.

As he began organizing everything, his eyes landed on the wooden box. He decided to take it apart to see if it also contained something hidden. He searched the drawers for tools and found a letter opener and a screwdriver.

Alright, let's give this a shot, he muttered to himself.

He sat down, carefully wedging the screwdriver into the seam, then followed with the letter opener. Slowly and gently, he worked the inner lining loose, mindful not to damage the wood. After some careful prying, it finally loosened. He turned the box over, tapping and shaking it lightly until the lining fell onto the table.

Then, focusing on the bottom panel, he pried at its edges until it popped free.

His jaw dropped. Beneath the panel was another hidden piece of paper—identical to the one he had found in the *Fennia's* box.

Heart pounding with hope, he quickly unfolded it. It was a letter from Hans to his wife, Greta, dated December 25, 1939.

Wasting no time, he opened his laptop to translate. This had to be one of those forbidden letters—the kind prisoners were never allowed to send because they contained classified information.

Like Karl's letter, which he had discovered in Paysandú, Hans recounted his experiences: the sinking of their ship, his rescue at sea by Karl Henning, and their perilous arrival at the islands in a small boat—the only two survivors of the mission.

Hans described their plan to escape to Argentina using a sailboat they had spotted at a nearby port, but their capture came before they could set sail. He also mentioned their subsequent imprisonment aboard the *Fennia*.

At the end of the letter, Hans revealed that he had found something important—something he had to hide as British forces closed in on them. His final words were a tender farewell and his signature.

"Wow," Víctor whispered. *This says it all. They found something important. Could it be the treasure— the legendary bounty of Patrick?*

He thought about it carefully. *Now I just have to find that place, but... how? Should I tell John everything I know?*

Víctor was conflicted, but he ultimately decided that he shouldn't share anything just yet. It was better to keep everything secret. The fewer people knew, the fewer problems there would be—especially while he was in foreign territory.

He snapped a photo of the letter, carefully placed it back in the box, and reassembled it, leaving it exactly as he had found it.

He decided to call Diana to find out when they could visit her friend and then head to Port Louis. With this new information, his sense of urgency grew even stronger. He knew something important was hidden somewhere, and he wanted to find it as soon as possible. His trip would end in less than a week, and he didn't want to leave the islands without discovering it.

As he pondered how time had now become his worst enemy, there was a knock at the door, which then opened gently.

"Hi! May I come in?" a soft, gentle voice floated through the slightly open doorway.

Víctor looked up from his notes, momentarily surprised, before recognizing the familiar warmth in the tone. He smiled. "Of course, come in."

The door creaked softly as Diana stepped inside, her eyes bright with curiosity and something else—anticipation, maybe. She lingered for a moment, taking in the scattered papers and open laptop on the desk, before finally meeting his gaze.

"Diana! What a surprise! I was just thinking about you. What are the odds?"

"Good thoughts, I hope?" she teased with a playful smirk.

"I was thinking about calling you… and yes, good things too."

"John told me to come up. Are you busy? I called the hotel, and they said you weren't there, so I figured I'd drop by. How's everything going?"

"Good—really good, actually. I'm making solid progress with the investigation. Come in, have a seat while I tidy this up. I was just about to call you, thinking of grabbing lunch and maybe heading to Port Louis."

"Lunch sounds perfect, Víctor, but Port Louis will have to wait till tomorrow. I spoke with Ashley—

she's expecting us then and seems excited I'm coming along."

"Really? That's great!" Víctor said, his voice filled with excitement.

"Yes, and they're saying it will be a beautiful day tomorrow, according to the weather folks. Surprisingly, there'll be little wind, and it'll be sunny. You'll feel better, I think."

"That's wonderful. I've had good news recently… and it's been a boost for me. I found some interesting details today."

"I'm glad to hear that. Oh, by the way, my friend has prepared a place for us to stay overnight—if that's okay with you."

"I hadn't thought about that, but now that you mention it, it might be a good idea. Honestly, I don't know what we'll discover there, but staying overnight would definitely give us more time."

"What do you want to discover?"

"Well, a journalist is always discovering things. I meant for the story."

"Ah, of course. As for lunch, there's a restaurant near the harbor. We can eat there."

"Sure, wherever you choose is fine. You know I don't know my way around. Oh, and afterward, I'd like to check out the old cargo ship *Lady Elizabeth*. It seems like a great spot to take some photos."

"Yeah, it's near there. You'll like it. Whenever you're ready, we can go. Also, I can show you the old airport, the lighthouse, the beach behind it and then we can stop by some of the battlefields from the 1982 war."

"Okay, that sounds really interesting. Let me put everything away, and I'm ready to go."

"Good, I'll head down and wait for you in John's office."

"Perfect."

When he finished organizing, Víctor left the room and went straight to the office. Diana was chatting animatedly with John when he walked in.

"John, I've tidied everything up. I'll come back another time if I need anything else. For now, I think I have enough material to write part of my story, for now."

"Of course, no problem at all."

"I invited him to lunch with us, but he can't come," Diana said.

"Are you sure? It would be great if you joined us," Víctor added.

"No, Liz is expecting me at home. Besides, I want to keep researching the ship. But thanks anyway—maybe another time, okay?"

"Alright, no problem. Well, Diana, I'm ready," Víctor said with a smile.

"Goodbye, have fun," John said. "I hope you enjoy our city. I'll keep searching for more information on the ship, and if I find anything, I'll let you know."

They exchanged goodbyes and left the museum.

Once outside, Diana asked, "What ship were you talking about?"

"A ghost. A ghost ship. I'll explain it to you later."

After lunch and a stroll around Stanley, they went to Whalebone Cove to see the *Lady Elizabeth,* a ship that ran aground in 1936. Víctor took several photos from afar, as the tide didn't allow him to get closer. Seeing that ship in that setting, helped him imagine the *Fennia* sailing those waters years ago. The *Lady Elizabeth* was older, built in 1879, with three masts and a length of sixty-seven meters, but its iron hull and design were very similar to *Fennia*.

From there, they visited Stanley Airport, the nearby lighthouse, drove by the beach and then toured the battlefields of Mount Longdon, Two Sisters, Mount Harriet, Tumbledown, and Wireless Ridge. Goose Green, Darwin, and San Carlos were farther away, so they decided to leave those for another day if time allowed.

Despite the breathtaking yet desolate landscape, visiting these places was a solemn experience. It was impossible not to imagine the events that had unfolded here so long ago—the young men on both sides, far from their homelands, their lives cut short in a conflict that left its mark on this distant land.

"It's such a shame that we, as humans, can't solve some problems without resorting to war. It doesn't make sense," Víctor said as they finished their tour and returned to Stanley.

"Yeah, it is. Over the past two years, living here, I've met many veterans of the war—both British and Argentines who visit occasionally. It's heartbreaking to hear their stories. This past June 14 marked the 35th anniversary of the conflict's end. Despite everything, as sad as it is to say, the war brought improvements to the islands in many ways," Diana said.

"Well, at least that's some consolation," Víctor replied.

"Yes, it is. Do you think the Falklands belong to Argentina?"

"Oh, no, Diana. Don't get me in trouble. I didn't come to the islands to discuss that," he said with a nervous laugh.

"Well, I know. But it's just a simple question. You must have some opinion on it. Surely you've researched or studied the history and the war."

"Yes, I have. Not extensively, but I've studied it a bit."

"And?" she pressed.

"Look, Diana. It's not for me to answer that—it's up to those who live here. There was a referendum in 2013, and they voted to remain under the British flag and administration."

"Yes, that's true. But you're still avoiding the question."

"I'm not. I believe the islanders should decide their future, not me. But I will say this: back then, the United Provinces of the Rio de la Plata were dealing with political instability, and the British seized the opportunity. It's been 149 years between that time and the war of 1982—184 years now. That's a long time. The best path forward is to live peacefully as neighbors, like brothers, and move on."

"Yes, I agree," Diana said quietly.

"Hey, and you? What do you think?" Víctor asked, turning the tables.

"Oh, are you trying to get me in trouble now? I live here," she teased.

"Come on, it's just the two of us. No one else can hear, and I promise I won't tell," Víctor said with a playful smile.

Diana smirked, then after a brief pause, she finally said, "I agree with you."

As they reached Stanley, the last rays of sunlight painted the undersides of the low-hanging clouds a deep crimson.

Exhausted from their intense day of climbing and hiking across the mountains, Diana took him straight to the hotel.

"That was a great tour, Diana. Even though some of the places we visited were sad, it was a wonderful experience—very informative and especially… very thought-provoking."

"I promise the next places won't be as sad. We still have a penguin colony, some more remote beaches, and other natural sites to visit. I just hope we have enough time. Despite being relatively small islands, there's so much to see."

Diana pulled into the hotel parking lot and stopped her Rover near the entrance.

"Yeah, I see. Anyway, rest well. Come early, and we can have breakfast here if you'd like before heading out."

"Yes, good idea. Hmm… tomorrow at seven, does that work for you?"

"Yes, perfect."

They exchanged a kiss on the cheek, and she gave him that familiar, mischievous wink. Víctor closed the door, waved with a smile, and stood there watching until the Rover disappeared from sight.

Back in his room, he packed his bag, making sure everything was ready for an early departure. He considered jotting down a few notes about the day's events but decided against it. A hot shower and sleep sounded far more appealing. He was exhausted. Better to wake up early, well-rested, and write with a clear mind before breakfast.

Chapter XII

Journey to Isthmus Camp

Víctor stopped by the front desk to let them know he'd be heading out to the countryside for a few days and would return on Friday or Saturday. Then, he made his way to the restaurant, which that morning was occupied by just two couples. He greeted them with a simple "Good morning," found a seat by one of the windows overlooking the bay, and sat down to wait for Diana.

The red acrylic lamps hanging over the tables cast a warm glow, slightly offsetting the chill of the southern winter outside. Víctor pulled out his notebook and pretended to review his notes. In truth, he already knew them by heart, but it gave him something to focus on, disguising his nervousness and impatience. He couldn't decide if it was the anticipation of possibly uncovering something significant that day or the excitement of seeing Diana again. Whatever it was, he felt a sense of contentment with everything happening around him.

A few minutes later, she arrived.

"Good morning, Víctor. You're up early." She greeted him with a kiss and a brief hug before sitting across from him.

"Hi, good morning. Yeah, can you believe it? I've been up for hours. Got out of bed around five. I wanted to get ahead in my writing... How about you?"

"No, not me," she replied with a laugh. "I don't write. Although... maybe someday—maybe someday—who knows?" she added, her gaze drifting toward some distant dream.

"Honestly, I almost stayed in bed. I was so exhausted from yesterday's hike that I hit the snooze button three times... but here I am, ready to go!" She grinned.

As they ate breakfast, their conversation was filled with exchanged glances and laughter. For reasons they couldn't quite explain, it felt as though they had known each other forever, despite being certain they had never met before. They talked about the journey ahead and the paths life had taken to bring them to this moment in their respective stories. They shared anecdotes of past loves and relationships, discussed the good and bad aspects of life in the Falklands, and reflected on how moving there had changed Diana's life."

A little after eight, they were leaving the hotel. They stopped at a gas station to fill the tank and pick up some supplies Ashley had requested, as well as snacks for the journey. Although their destination was only about 40 kilometers away, the trip would take longer because they planned to stop at several interesting points along the way to take photos.

And so they did. Víctor was particularly captivated by a place called Princess Street Stone Run, which resembled a colossal stone causeway. It stretched four kilometers long and 400 meters wide. The site had been named by Charles Darwin when he visited the islands in 1833 during his voyage aboard the *HMS Beagle*. He had been reminded of Princess Street in Edinburgh, Scotland's capital, due to its resemblance to the cobblestone streets there.

After a brief walk and taking some photos, they continued on their way until they reached the entrance to Isthmus Camp, near Berkeley Sound. They paused there to appreciate the area and to look at the entire inlet from that vantage point. Víctor thought he caught sight of the town of Port Louis in the distance, snapped a few photos, and they resumed their journey. At that moment, he realized he had forgotten to call for the permits needed to visit the site. He hoped the Smiths, being locals, could help them out.

When they arrived at the main homestead, two friendly collies greeted them before anyone else, barking and wagging their tails at them. The property was expansive, featuring several houses spread apart, along with barns and pens for sheep and cattle. When they parked in front of the main house — a white-walled building with a red gabled roof, surrounded by a vast treeless yard typical of the island, two women stepped onto the porch, wiping their hands on aprons, followed closely by a little girl, no older than eight. The moment she spotted Diana, her face lit up, and she dashed forward.

Diana knelt to catch her, scooping her up effortlessly with a warm smile before planting a kiss on her cheek.

After exchanging greetings between them, Diana turned around and introduced Víctor, who was waiting patiently a little further back.

"Hi, good morning, ladies!" Víctor said.

"Hello," the young woman responded. "I'm Ashley. Nice to meet you. This is my daughter, Antonina — we call her Nina — and my mom, Amelia."

"It's a pleasure to meet you," Víctor replied, shaking their hands. "Thank you for having me."

"The pleasure is ours. Please, come inside," Ashley said.

Víctor and Diana grabbed their luggage and the boxes of provisions they'd picked up, following the women inside.

The house was large, L-shaped, and single-story. Amelia excused herself to the kitchen, mentioning she had something on the stove, while Ashley led them to their respective rooms to drop off their belongings.

Once they were settled, everyone gathered in the main living room.

"Paul is out in the field," Amelia said. "He'll be back this afternoon. He was thrilled when I told him you were coming, Diana. We've missed you around here."

"I've missed you too. It's been a while since my last visit," Diana said.

"Yes, since you and Ashley started classes. Now we'll have time to catch up on everything."

After a pleasant chat full of news and gossip, Víctor began explaining his intent to write an article about the story of Patrick and Annadee.

"We're honored that you want to write about our ancestors," Ashley said. "Professor McIntyre did some research on that era and the mysterious disappearance of Patrick, but since he couldn't uncover what happened, he left it unfinished."

"Yes, I know," Víctor replied. "He told me about it. But well, I actually came across your ancestor through a different investigation I was working on. My initial intention wasn't about him or your grandmother."

"Oh, wasn't it? Then what?" Ashley asked, confused.

"Well... it seems that this story involves a series of events that have occurred over many years and are somehow interconnected, leading me to discover their existence. I'm not sure why, but it feels like destiny placed me on this path for a reason... somewhat mysterious, you could say."

"Life's twists and turns are always mysterious, Mr. Cabot," Ashley commented. "There's a thread that connects all of us in the end."

"Yes, I believe you're right about that. Anyway, in the days I spent with the professor, he briefed me on some of the events. I hope to build on his research and uncover more. I have a small theory based on the investigation I've been conducting from Uruguay, but I still need more evidence to determine if I'm on the right track. That's why I need more information. Also, I wanted to visit the places where they lived and spent their time."

"Well, no problem. We can do that. That place is close by."

"Yes, I know. I had already planned to come to this area. That was the original plan, but I didn't know there were relatives here, let alone living so close."

"Of course, you wouldn't have known," Amelia said. "It happened so many years ago. Patrick and Annadee lived nearby for a time. But when she returned to the islands in 1847, she went straight to Stanley, which had become the new capital. She never lived in Port Louis again."

"But why?" Ashley asked, leaning forward. "Why are you so interested in what happened to them so many years ago? Why this story, when there might be others that are perhaps more intriguing?"

"That's exactly what I wonder too," Amelia added. "Why this one?"

Víctor chuckled softly. "You know... I ask myself the same thing. I didn't choose this story. I think it chose me. I can't explain it any better than that. I simply stumbled upon pieces of information that led me here. Fate? Coincidence? I don't know. But here I am."

"Fate is wise sometimes," Diana said with a gentle smile.

"Would it be too much to ask," Víctor continued, "for you to tell me what you know about Patrick and Annadee's life?"

Amelia nodded thoughtfully. "We know the story — it's been passed down through generations. But it's a sad one... a story without an ending. Poor Annadee suffered greatly. After her parents passed away in Uruguay in 1847, she returned here, hoping to find Patrick. But she never heard from him again."

Ashley added, "Her parents died just months apart. She was left alone with her daughter, so she came back. But as for Patrick, after he disappeared, nothing more was ever heard of him."

"That's exactly what I'm trying to uncover," Víctor said. "I need to know what happened to him. That's why I'm here."

Amelia gave him a small smile. "All right, I'll tell you the story. But first, let's have lunch. The food is ready, and I think Nina is getting hungry. Aren't you, my little darling?"

"Yes, Grandma," Nina replied eagerly. "But you have to tell the story after!"

"Of course, Nina. It's time you learned about our ancestors."

"You always tell me stories, Grandma, but never that one," Nina pouted.

"You're right, sweetheart. I'll tell you after lunch. Now go wash your hands."

Lunch served as a time to get to know each other better. They discovered their mutual love for rural life. Víctor shared stories from his youth as a rural producer before life pulled him in another direction. Diana recalled her childhood on her parents' farm outside Mercedes before moving to Montevideo for her studies. The Smiths, too, had built their lives in the countryside. Paul and Amelia had met as teenagers in Stanley during secondary school, married young, and spent forty years together, raising their daughter and granddaughter at the camp.

After clearing the table, they gathered in the living room with cups of tea, settling near the peat-burning stove. Víctor stared at it, fascinated. He had never seen anything like it — to him, it looked like they were burning plain soil.

Chapter XIII

What Happened in 1829
Puerto Soledad

"This story begins on a very cold winter's day, perhaps much like today. On July 14, 1829, to be exact. On that day, a brig named *Betsy* arrived in these waters, commanded by Matthew Brisbane."

"What's a brig, Grandma?" Nina asked with great interest.

"Well, it's a sailing ship, like the ones from *Pirates of the Caribbean*. Remember the movie we watched?"

"Yes, I remember... Were they pirates?"

"No, my dear. They weren't. But let me finish the story, and I'll explain anything you don't understand afterward, okay?"

"Okay, sure. Later."

"Thank you, Nina."

"Well, as I was saying: The Betsy carried several passengers. In total, about twenty-three families of various nationalities. These new settlers were heading to the islands with Luis Vernet, a German-born resident of Buenos Aires, his wife María Saez Pérez—who was born in Montevideo and was two months pregnant—and their three children: Luis Emilio, Luisa, and Sofía. Vernet had been appointed as the new governor by Manuel Dorrego and the government of the United Provinces of the Rio de la Plata.

The day after they arrived, they disembarked at *Puerto Soledad*. This port has had several names over the years: Port Saint Louis, *Puerto Soledad*, Puerto Luis, Anson Harbor, and Port Louis. It was founded by the French in 1764 and later came under Spanish control in 1767.

They all arrived full of dreams and hopes, eager to start a new life on the islands. Among them were our ancestors: Alexander Bauer, his wife Marie Anne Fischer-Bauer, and their 16-year-old daughter, Annadee. The settlement, *Puerto Soledad*, as it was called at the time, was not quite what Luis Vernet had promised the settlers it would be. No, it was very different. But the Bauers didn't mind; after all, it was a new place, and every beginning is difficult. On the other hand, this gave them many advantages and opportunities.

At that time, the port was bustling with maritime activity due to its proximity to Cape Horn, a key crossing for many trade routes. Ships also stopped there for whaling, seal and sea lion hunting, and to make repairs, replenish water, meat, and other supplies—either for their crew and passengers or to trade with other ports. Despite its small population of about one hundred at the time, it was a promising place.

Annadee's parents settled in well, but at first, she wasn't very happy, as she noted in her journal. The isolation affected her the most, being on an island far from everything and from her friends in Montevideo. But gradually, she adjusted to island life—its work, the neighbors and new friends, and the ships that came and went. After all, it was a peaceful place. And while the winters were harsh, summers could be quite pleasant.

Many settlers came and stayed, while others left disappointed because they didn't find what they were seeking or had been promised. And so it was that, amidst this flow of settlers, passengers, and sailors, one day, exactly two years later, the brig *Elbe* arrived.

This ship had departed from the port of Montevideo on June 26, 1831, carrying more settlers to the Falklands Islands, arriving at *Puerto Soledad* on July 15th.

Among the crew members of the *Elbe* was a young and handsome sailor named Patrick Sans McGowan. He claimed he wasn't planning to stay. His port job was simply to unload the cargo they carried in the hold and load up supplies: water and food for the crew, passengers, and perhaps freight destined for another port. Afterward, he would continue his journey without looking back.

The ship was anchored at *Puerto Soledad* for several days while everything was gathered and loaded into the hold. One of those days, while working onshore, Patrick took the opportunity to visit William Dickinson's store near the dock to buy a knife, as he had lost his during the voyage. It was on that very day, in the town store, that they saw each other for the first time. He was entering just as she was leaving. That was the moment their lives and destinies changed forever.

Patrick, well-mannered and ever the gentleman, held the door open for her as she passed. 'Good morning, miss,' he said as he removed his hat, made a slight bow, and stood there, mesmerized by her beauty. Annadee only gave a slight nod of acknowledgment, a fleeting glance, and continued on her way with her mother. She immediately noticed that the young man was not from there, as she knew all the inhabitants of the town. She assumed he was either a passing sailor or a passenger from one of the newly arrived ships.

Another ship, the *Harriet*, an American whaling vessel, had arrived alongside the *Elbe*. Consequently, the days at *Puerto Soledad* were bustling with new faces. This ship, which would soon play a significant role in the coming changes to the island's history, had been in the area for some time, hunting and fishing."

"Were they your grandparents, Grandma?" asked Antonina, her eyes wide with fascination and fully engrossed in the story.

"Yes, and yours too. It's a story full of grandparents, you see?"

"Yes! Well, keep going, don't stop."

"Well then, young lady, if you don't interrupt me," she said with a laugh.

"As I was saying, this young man, Patrick, was about nineteen years old at the time. He had decided to travel the world by ship, but that day, mesmerized by Annadee's beauty, he realized that staying on solid ground might be the wisest choice. When they later became friends, he shared with her that he had boarded the ship in Montevideo. His mother, an Irishwoman, had passed away when he was just a child, and his father, a stern Spaniard with whom he didn't get along well, took him to live on a farm in northern *Banda Oriental*.

When Patrick turned eighteen, he left home, and as soon as he could secure work on a ship, he did so without hesitation. He told Annadee he had wanted to see the world, but when he saw her blue eyes in this land far from his own, they captivated him more than the sea ever could. In her gaze, he felt he could see all the oceans and all the skies. And he thought that perhaps this was what he had set out to find.

Annadee found him quite handsome as well. She adored his kindness and gentlemanly manners, his way of being, his sense of humor, and his confidence. The captain of the *Elbe* wasn't particularly surprised when Patrick told him he intended to stay in these lands. 'I'd do the same at your age,' the captain said. 'She seems like a fine young woman. But do you think she'll return your affection?'

Patrick replied, 'I don't know, Captain, but I think it's worth finding out. I wouldn't be much use on board if I spent my days wondering what could have been had I stayed behind. Besides, I know the *Elbe* and you will sail these waters again someday. By then, I'll know whether I made the right choice. And it's a good place to settle—these fields remind me somewhat of the countryside of Banda Oriental. I believe I can have a good future here,' he said with confidence, gazing at the town from the *Elbe's* deck. 'I'll make this a good place to call home.'

'Don't worry, son,' said the captain, placing a hand on Patrick's shoulder. 'If, when I return, you want to come back aboard, you'll be welcome.'

The captain allowed Patrick to keep working on the ship for a few more days. After unloading everything destined for the island, they began loading cowhides, seal pelts, dried meat, and several live animals. Patrick also did some carpentry work and repairs to the sails. He wasn't entirely sure where or how he'd find work once he left the ship, so he needed to save as much money as possible—whether in silver or gold—to support himself for a while in *Puerto Soledad.*

Before departing, the captain personally recommended Patrick to the townspeople as a responsible, friendly, intelligent, and well-educated young man. 'That should help you land a good job. Good luck, son!' he said, gave him a hug, and left.

"The other sailors from the *Elbe,* still onshore, shook his hand and jokingly told him that he'd soon be on the first ship out of those islands, sailing away and free of troubles with women.

Thanks to the captain's recommendations, Patrick quickly found work—and, even better, with the Bauer family. His initial tasks included building a shed, a stone corral, and working on the land with other *gauchos*, rounding up wild cattle, much like the *vaquerías* of his native *Banda Oriental.*

By that time, the port was bustling with people—English, Spanish, German, French, gauchos, and a few Charrúa, Guaraní, and Tehuelche natives. There were more men than women. Most were from rural backgrounds, but there was also a baker, builders, a stoneworker, a blacksmith, carpenters, sailors, and a few soldiers.

The town at that time had a Catholic church, a small hospital with a doctor, a fort with four cannons, a general store, a bakery, a blacksmith shop, a central plaza, vegetable gardens. On the outskirts, a circular stone corral and the cemetery. At the cove, there was a pier, two rowboats, and two small sailing vessels used for fishing and seal hunting to supply *Puerto Soledad*. Among the domestic animals were cattle, sheep, geese, chickens, pigs, and horses that had been brought to the Falkland Islands during the early days of colonization.

Two streams ran on either side of the town, providing fresh water, which was very clear and delicious. For firewood, the settlers used shrubs, straw, and peat, as there were no trees on the islands. Peat was abundant—it only needed to be cut and left to dry in the sun before use. Much of the wood for construction and repairs was brought from *Patagonia* or *Isla de los Estados*.

The fields, except for the rocky areas of the hills and mountains, were covered with tussock grass and other shrubs. That hasn't changed much—the landscape looks nearly the same today.

Fifteen days after Patrick arrived in the Falkland Islands, on July 30, 1831, the *Harriet*, the American ship that had arrived the same day as the *Elbe* and was captained by Gilbert Davison, was confiscated by Governor Luis Vernet under accusations of illegal hunting. Two other American ships, the *Superior*, captained by Stephen Congar, and the *Breakwater*, captained by Daniel Carew, would later be seized under similar accusations. This event would change history, though no one suspected it at the time.

Meanwhile, the bond between the Bauer family and Patrick grew so strong that they treated him as one of their own—though Annadee certainly didn't see him as a brother. For them, it had been love at first sight. Patrick and Annadee became close friends from the beginning.

Their first conversation happened when Annadee saw Patrick working in the shed. She had gone to fetch some candles stored there and to collect eggs from the hen's nests. Seeing him there, she quietly approached from behind, unnoticed, as he was busy engraving something into the silver and gold handle of the knife he had bought at Dickinson's store.

Just then, a hen suddenly flew out of one of the nests, flapping its wings wildly and kicking up a cloud of dust as it clucked loudly. Startled, Annadee let out a loud scream, which in turn startled Patrick, causing him to jump aside. Once they realized what had happened, both burst into laughter, unable to stop for several moments. Each time they tried to compose themselves, they would catch each other's eye and start laughing again.

When they finally calmed down, he approached her, removed his tricorn hat, and formally introduced himself:

'Hello, my name is Patrick. Patrick Sans McGowan.'

'Yes, I know. I'm Annadee. Annadee Bauer Fischer. A pleasure,' she said, extending her hand, which he kissed. 'I came for some candles and got scared by that crazy chicken.'

'That chicken gave us quite a fright,' Patrick said with a chuckle. 'For a moment, I thought it was the chicken screaming until I saw you.'

'How funny! And what were you doing?' she asked curiously

'Oh, nothing much, just carving my name into my new knife. But look at this,' he said, showing her the handle. 'When I jumped, I made this deep scratch. It won't be easy to fix. But oh well, it's fine. I'll remember this moment every time I see it.'

'Oh, I'm so sorry! But is that a good thing or a bad thing? I mean, remembering this moment?' she asked playfully.

'Well, I'd say it was lovely and... funny, Miss Bauer.'

'I'm glad. It was for me too, Mr. Sans,' she replied, realizing she was blushing.

Wanting to escape the awkward moment and unsure of what else to say, she repeated her reason for coming. Patrick nodded and helped her retrieve the candles hanging from the ceiling before gathering the eggs from the nests. With their hands full and their laughter still lingering in the air, they exchanged polite farewells and returned to their tasks, each carrying the memory of their unexpected encounter.

That was the beginning of their beautiful relationship, though for a long time, neither dared to express their feelings for the other. Whenever they could, they spent time together, although Annadee also helped her mother greatly with household chores. She worked in the kitchen, tended the garden, milked cows, made butter and cheese, crafted candles, fed the chickens, and gathered eggs. Additionally, she took piano lessons from María Saez Pérez, the wife of Governor Luis Vernet.

Patrick, on the other hand, taught her many skills he had learned in the countryside of *Banda Oriental,* such as horseback riding, lassoing, and wielding *boleadoras*. On days they managed to slip away, they explored the mountains, coastline, and beaches. They went hunting, fishing, or collecting mussels on the shore. There was always something interesting to do or see since they both loved to explore, whether on foot or horseback.

Feeling happy and content on the island, Patrick decided to purchase a plot of land in town from Luis Vernet within a month of his arrival, using his savings. He planned to build something there later. Annadee was thrilled by this since it assured her that Patrick wouldn't be leaving on another ship, as Antonina Roxa, a resident of Port Louis and a family friend, had once suggested.

On Thursday, November 24, 1831, as Annadee recounts in her diary, during one of their horseback outings, they visited a beach they both loved and decided to stay for a few hours, observing penguins and the few remaining seals."

'There are hardly any seals left on the coast,' Annadee said, concerned. 'Nor are there sea lions or elephant seals. Have you noticed, Patrick? I think Don Luis Vernet is right to regulate hunting. The whalers don't even respect when whales are pregnant or with young calves. They hunt everything, even our cattle. That's why he left to sort those matters in Buenos Aires. He must already be there. We'll hear news soon.'"

At this point, Amelia paused the story about Annadee and Patrick to explain to Víctor that Governor Luis Vernet had traveled to Buenos Aires with his family aboard the schooner *Harriet* to bring the captain and crew of the other confiscated ships to trial for illegal hunting and fishing. They arrived in Buenos Aires on November 19, 1831. Poaching was decimating sea lions and seals and also endangering the *guará*, or warrah, a species of wild dog native to the islands, now extinct. The last one of its kind was killed in 1876.

After this brief explanation, Amelia resumed the story exactly where she had left off, in the middle of a conversation:

"'I don't know, Annadee; I hadn't realized. Don't forget I've only been here four months. What was it like before? Were there more? Can you notice the difference?' Patrick asked, playing along.

'Yes, quite a bit. The *gauchos* also say they see sailors hunting on the coast with no regard for control. The townspeople notice it too when ships bring pelts to trade for food, gunpowder, or musket bullets,' Annadee explained.

'Well, then I think having controls in place, as *Don* Luis wants, is a good idea. But without a strong detachment or enough ships for patrols, there's little he can do. Don't you think? The military fort we have doesn't scare anyone. There aren't many soldiers. And the islands are so large that Luis Vernet can't possibly monitor everything with what the Buenos Aires government provides him. There are plenty of places to hide or hunt without being seen. It almost seems like the United Provinces government doesn't care much,' Patrick said, now sounding somewhat concerned.

'I see you're quite interested in the matters of *Puerto Soledad*, Patrick.'

'Of course, I'm interested. I care deeply about the future of *Islas Malvinas*. It's also our future, Annadee. You know how much I love this place. I chose it to live in, and I want to protect it as best I can, but maybe I shouldn't get into this.

'I care too, but I don't want to get involved either—it's not a woman's affair. But I believe it's possible to live well in this place, especially with you since you make everything more beautiful. I don't need anything else.'

Patrick, surprised by Annadee's frank words, wanted to avert his gaze but knew it was time to tell her how he felt. He had known her for only four months, yet it felt like a lifetime. Patrick moved closer, took her hand, brought it to his lips, and kissed it. It was a longer kiss than he usually gave her. She blushed and could no longer look him in the eyes when he finished. He let go of her hand and stepped even closer. Annadee instinctively tried to step back, but her nerves betrayed her. She wanted to speak, but no words came—her pounding heart and ragged breath made thinking clearly impossible.

Patrick hesitated before kissing her on the lips. He loved this woman but wasn't sure if she felt the same, despite their friendship, and he didn't want to lose that. Gently, he lifted her chin and brushed his thumb across her red lips. Annadee raised her eyes to meet his green ones and softly kissed his fingers. Then, lowering her hand, she brought her face closer to his.

Neither of them could pull away now. The passion was overwhelming, and as their lips touched and parted in a passionate kiss, the only words they stopped to exchange were: 'I love you.' They smiled as they said it and embraced tightly."

"What a beautiful love story," Diana sighed.

"That was one of the most cherished moments Grandma remembered. From the time she returned to the island until her death, she visited that beach every November 24th. It's a small beach that emerges at low tide, connecting to an islet in Berkeley Sound," Amelia explained.

There was a brief pause as everyone enjoyed their tea before Amelia continued the couple's story:

"'Thank you, Annadee,' Patrick said. 'We will be very happy together, with lots of children running after penguins, and us playing with them.'

She laughed.

'That will be a funny sight... But see, that's why I want to take care of this place. It's where we met. Of all the places in the world, we crossed paths here. It's one of those life events, you know? This is where we'll build our family.'

'Yes, we will, Annadee. We will,' Patrick repeated.

They remained locked in each other's embrace, gazing into one another's eyes, stroking each other's faces, and listening to the endless waves—waves that seemed to mirror the unending nature of their love. As the afternoon wore on, they took their horses by the reins and started walking back toward the setting sun.

As they walked, Patrick mentioned the issues he'd noticed:

'About the hunters, these islands still don't have a defined or strong government, which is why hunting and fishing are chaotic.'

'True. And we also have the English claiming this as their territory,' Annadee said.

'But they don't seem to be doing much, do they? It's like this place belongs to everyone and no one at the same time. In other places where there were native populations—land already inhabited—they've been displaced, as is happening with the natives in *Banda Oriental* or the United Provinces. But these islands, which could be fully colonized with little effort, don't seem to worry them much,' Patrick added.

'You're right. It would be easier to settle these islands, but they don't do much. If it weren't for *Don* Luis Vernet, this would truly be *terra nullius*. I don't understand the rulers. Someday, someone will take this colony seriously, and then problems will come. By then, it'll be too late.'

'I think you're right, Annadee. But tell me, what do you foresee for the future? What would you like to happen?'

'Oh, well, many things. It's still a relatively new place. Years ago, there was an English port on another island to the west—Port Egmont, I think it was called. That's why I believe these islands could attract more settlers from all over. Or maybe the other big island could be for the English and this one for the United Provinces—cooperation instead of conflict. Trade here looks promising; it's a key point for ships passing through Cape Horn. Who knows? Maybe one day, it could even become an independent country. But for now, we still rely heavily on Montevideo and Buenos Aires.'

'You're right. *Elbe's* Captain used to say the same. Without these islands as supply points, voyages would be much harder and more dangerous. Aside from that, what do you think will happen with the American ships *Don* Vernet seized? I'm worried they'll rebel against our new laws. If they did, we couldn't defend ourselves.'

'Don't worry. Even though some rumors call *Don* Luis's seizure of those ships piracy, it's not true. Many good people want to work and progress in peace. Everything will turn out fine, you'll see. And now that we're together, let's enjoy this moment and be happy. I love you, Patrick. Thank you for coming to *Islas Malvinas!*'

'And I love you, Annadee. Thank you for being here.'

They embraced and kissed."

"And that's how it was," Amelia said. "They loved each other deeply and were very happy together. It seemed like they had everything and it would only get better, but their happiness was destined to be cut short. Fate wouldn't align with their desires and dreams. Unfortunately, Luis Vernet's actions in seizing the *Harriet*, the *Superior*, and the *Breakwater* triggered reactions that would forever change the life of *Puerto Soledad*, its inhabitants, and the Falkland Islands."

Chapter XIV

The discovery of the Liberty Rose

"You know, Nina, your Grandpa Patrick once found a ghost ship washed up on the coast—with a treasure inside."

Nina's eyes widened in astonishment, her curiosity instantly piqued.

"Really, Grandma?"

Nina turned to her mom and asked, "Did you hear that, Mom? Did you know?"

"Yes, incredible, isn't it?" Ashley replied, though she knew it was just a legend, as there was never any proof of such a ship or the supposed treasure.

"Did they really find a treasure, Grandma?" Nina asked eagerly.

Paul, who had just returned from the fields and entered the house unnoticed, answered the question:

"Yes, and also a little mermaid as pretty as you, Nina. How are you?" he said as he lifted her into his arms.

"Hi, Grandpa. Where were you? Do you know this story too?"

"Yes, I do. Hi, Diana, it's so good to see you here again!"

He then turned to Víctor.

"And who might this gentleman be?"

"Víctor Cabot, sir. A pleasure to meet you."

"Ah, the journalist from Uruguay. Welcome. How are you?"

"Very well, sir, thank you. Enjoying your family's stories."

Impatient, Nina tugged at her grandfather's chin to make him look at her.

"But mermaids don't exist, Grandpa. That's just in stories and movies. I've never seen one at the beach. Just seals... and seagulls... and penguins."

Grandpa chuckled. "Well, maybe we just haven't been looking in the right places. One day, we'll go searching for them. Who knows? We might get lucky and spot one. What do you think?"

"Okay, Grandpa. As you wish. But Grandma, tell me! Did they really find mermaids and treasure on the ship?" she asked, eyes wide with excitement.

Grandma smiled. "No mermaids, my love, but yes—he did find a treasure. Or at least, that's what he told Annadee. It happened near Volunteer Point, back in December of 1831, according to his story. Do you remember when we went there to see the penguins? That's Volunteer Point."

Nina nodded eagerly.

"Well, no one ever knew exactly what happened. The ship disappeared the next day. They said the tides carried it back out to sea. Anyway, I can't remember the name of the ship..."

Víctor interrupted:

"Liberty Rose?"

Amelia's eyes widened. "Liberty Rose? Yes, that's it. But... how do you know?"

"Just something I came across in my research," Víctor said carefully.

He considered telling her everything right then and there but decided against it. Not yet. He needed to hear her version of events first—to piece together the full story before revealing what he knew.

"Well, thank you, Víctor. Shall I continue?"

"Yes!" Nina exclaimed.

Chapter XV

The Chest

Amelia took a deep breath and, with a gesture signaling Nina to stay quiet, resumed her story:

"Well, after a storm with hurricane-force winds and rain, Patrick was ordered to check the fields and inspect the cattle on the San Luis Peninsula, north and east of the harbor. The other gauchos headed south, so he had to go alone. They all departed at dawn, hoping to cover as much land as possible and return before nightfall. Patrick began in the north and worked his way east across the peninsula. Almost finished with his route, in the afternoon, he passed Cape Carysfort heading to Volunteer Point, when in the distance, behind the cliff, he spotted a mast with tattered sails hanging from it. *The storm must have driven it onto the island*, he thought. Climbing to the top of the cliff, he took in the sight below. A black frigate, its hull marked by a white stripe stretching from bow to stern, lay stranded against the rocky shore. The ship, roughly thirty to forty meters in length, bore the unmistakable design of an English vessel. From his vantage point,

Patrick had a clear view of the entire deck, but he saw no crew aboard. Patrick called out, his voice carried away by the wind, but there was no answer. Only the sound of waves crashing against the hull and the whistle of the wind tearing through the shredded sails reached his ears. He rode along the coast, heading south at first. In the distance, he caught sight of another ship, but before he could get a better look, it disappeared behind the mountains along the southern shore of Berkeley Sound. Turning north, he searched for any sign of survivors but found nobody. When Patrick returned to the shipwreck, he realized there was no flag raised, leaving him no clue about the ship's origin or allegiance. The sails were in tatters, the rigging had collapsed and no longer supported the three masts. Only one mast remained intact, while the other two were shattered. The frigate had around twenty cannons below deck and four carronades on the upper deck. Part of the hull was still floating, but the bow was lodged against the rocky shoreline, positioned perpendicular to the coast. Patrick called out several more times, but with no reply, he decided to go around the cliff, descend to the beach, and board the ship. He tied his horse to one of the ropes dangling from the bow and used another one to climb onto the deck. Cautiously and without haste, he made his way through the vessel toward the captain's cabin, hoping to find someone— or something—that could explain what had happened and to whom this frigate belonged. On the starboard rail, he noticed sections missing; parts of the sails hung limply over the edge, as if a sea monster had taken a bite out of them. If he could find the ship's logbook, he might learn where it came from, what it carried, or where it was heading. Upon reaching the cabin, he found only chaos. The windows were open, their shattered glass rattling as the wind and the ship's movements dictated. Large bloodstains covered the floor, suggesting something more than a storm had occurred. It was clear several people had walked across the area, leaving tracks that told a grim story. One stain indicated someone had been dragged toward a window, likely thrown into the sea. *This wasn't the work of a storm or a sea creature*, he thought. *This ship was attacked—or there was a mutiny. Could it have something to do with the ship I saw sailing away a while ago?* Patrick searched the ship for the logbook but found nothing. There were no weapons, no sabers, no pistols or muskets onboard. *They must have taken everything of value they could carry and left the ship to drift. Damn pirates. They looted it and probably killed everyone*, he thought. When he inspected the damaged rail, he realized the marks were caused by cannonballs. The shots had brought down the rigging, shredded the sails, and broken the masts. Without its sails, the frigate had been an easy target. Likely believing the ship would sink soon, they abandoned it. Patrick went back to the cabin to see if he could spot the ship's name on the stern through the windows. No matter how far he leaned, he couldn't make it out. *I'll find a way to learn its name. Ah, the bell—it should be there*, he thought. He quickly climbed up to the helm deck, but the bell was missing, as was the compass. A cannonball had completely torn them away. Furthermore, it was clear the pirates had taken their time and looted almost everything of value from the ship. Only the cannons— likely too heavy to carry—and the stern lanterns remained. Although the lanterns were partially torn from their mounts, they still clung to the deck. The chests in the cabin had been smashed, the mattresses shredded, and the cushions sliced in two. Patrick descended into the hold but found only small, worthless items. The powder magazine was empty. The only thing left to do was fetch a cart and salvage whatever he could: ropes, sails, wood—anything that remained and could be removed from the ship. Especially the cannons, which would be perfect for the fort. Everything held value on the islands, and shipwrecks always brought wood—an invaluable resource in a treeless place—perhaps even material for his future house. Thinking he could claim the wreck, he kept searching for more clues. As he walked below deck near the officer's cabin, a tapping sound stopped him in his tracks. *Someone injured?* He hurried toward the noise, but as soon as he entered the room, it ceased. He froze, startled and apprehensive. The ship rocked under the waves, the wood creaked, and the tapping resumed. 'Hello? Is someone there?' he called out, but only silence replied. Now more alarmed, Patrick drew his knife. The tapping continued. It was something loose, swaying and hitting the wall with the ship's movement. Yet, though the sound was right in front of him, he couldn't see its source. He listened closely, searching for the source of the rhythmic, persistent tapping. It seemed to come from inside a cabinet built into the wall. Patrick pressed his ear to the surface and listened intently.

Standing to the side, knife ready, he cautiously opened the door. Light spilled inside—empty.

What on earth is making that sound? he wondered.

The ship shifted again. The noise repeated. Patrick placed his hand on the inner wall, waiting for the next lurch. Then he found it. Tapping the wall with his knuckles, he heard a hollow echo.

There's something hidden back here! he thought, triumphant.

He tried to move the cabinet, but it was firmly built into the wall. While attempting to remove the panel covering the hollow area, his hand accidentally pressed against a small, protruding slat on one side. As he pushed it, there was a distinct click, and a hidden compartment sprang open.

A clever hiding place—this must hold something important, he murmured. *The pirates seem to have missed this spot, unlike the captain's cabin. Could this be what they were searching for?*

The hiding spot was a hollow carved into a block of oak, which had been embedded into the ship's hull. The cabinet had concealed the entire area. Inside, Patrick found a bottle of rum—the source of the tapping—a pistol with a powder horn and bullets, some papers, and a wooden chest lined with copper plating.

He set aside the rum, the pistol, and the papers, then dragged the chest until it fell to the floor. The weight filled Patrick with excitement. As he longed to marry Annadee, perhaps this would help him financially. With it, he could buy land, a ship, or start a salting business—anything to secure a better life for his beloved and himself.

The chest was slightly larger than a powder keg, with bronze handles on its sides and a latch secured by a padlock on the front. Engraved on the lid was the name *Liberty Rose*.

Could this be the name of the ship? Patrick wondered. When he tugged at the padlock, it opened effortlessly, as though it had only been fastened to hold the lid shut. His hopes plummeted.

It's probably empty, he thought.

But when he lifted the lid, his eyes lit up.

'Gold!' he exclaimed out loud.

Inside the chest were several gold bars, silver bars, coins, a golden cross adorned with emeralds, and an enormous gold chain. He couldn't believe his luck— he was rich! At least, for the moment. He knew that if the rightful owner surfaced, he would have no choice but to return it.

That thought sobered him, and he decided not to dwell on it. The best course of action was to leave the ship, figure out what to do next, learn more about the vessel, and then make a decision.

He secured the pistol at his waist, sheathed his knife, gathered the papers, and placed them inside the chest along with the bottle of rum. Before leaving the ship, he made one final inspection, combing the vessel from stern to bow to ensure no one was injured or in need of help.

Satisfied, he returned to the chest, hoisted it onto the deck, and dragged it to the bow. After one last glance at the ship, he tied the chest with a rope and lowered it to the beach.

The sun had just set behind the horizon when Patrick arrived at the Bauer estate. He unsaddled *Oriental*, his horse, and went to speak with his employer to report everything that had happened during his day. Despite his excitement about discovering the ship, he decided to first finish recounting his day's tasks before mentioning his find."

Amelia paused to add a touch of drama to the story and then launched directly into the dialogue between Patrick and his boss:

'Don Alexander, there's something else. I found a shipwreck.'

Alexander, who had just taken a sip of his evening tea, set his cup down with a sharp clink. His eyes narrowed as he studied Patrick's expression. 'What did you say, Patrick? Where?'

'Along the coast, near *Punta Voluntario*. It's a frigate.'

Alexander leaned forward, his brows furrowing. 'But... what frigate? Whose is it?'

'I don't know. I've never seen it in this port or any others. There were no flags, no name on the stern—at least, none I could see.'

Alexander inhaled deeply, his fingers tapping the wooden table. 'God help us... We must go and see if there are survivors.'

Patrick shook his head. 'No need, Don Alexander. I checked the entire frigate—there's no one there. No bodies, no signs of life.' He hesitated before lowering his voice. 'But there was blood. A lot of it.'

A heavy silence settled between them. The wind outside rattled the shutters, filling the room with a ghostly whisper.

'Blood?' Alexander finally said, crossing himself.

Patrick nodded grimly. 'Yes. This wasn't the work of a storm. The ship was attacked—or there was a mutiny. The damage to the hull wasn't from the rocks. I saw cannon holes and splintered wood. Whoever was on that ship... they didn't abandon it willingly.'

Alexander exhaled sharply, rubbing his temple. 'Poor souls, may God have mercy on them.'

Patrick nodded. 'Amen.' He hesitated before adding, 'There's something else. As I stood on the cliff, I spotted a ship on the horizon heading south. I can't say for sure if it's connected, but the timing...'

Alexander's expression darkened. 'That's not a coincidence, Patrick.' He paused before glancing at the flickering lantern between them. 'We'll go at first light with the men and see what we can uncover. But Patrick, if this is what it seems, there could be danger. Whoever did this might still be watching.'

Patrick swallowed, a chill running down his spine—not from the cold, but from the weight of Alexander's words.

'One more thing, Don Alexander," he said cautiously. "If no one claims the wreck... do you think I could?"

Alexander studied him for a long moment before answering. 'That depends. You'll need to speak with Vernet when he returns or with Metcalf in the meantime. But first, we need to know what happened on that ship.' He gave Patrick a pointed look. 'No one lays claim to a ghost ship without first understanding its ghosts.'

Patrick suggested bringing a cart with tools. Perhaps they could repair the ship enough to bring it in by water. If not, they could at least recover some items to transport overland. However, he didn't mention the chest of gold. He preferred to wait for another moment to bring it up."

Chapter XVI

What Happened to the Frigate?

Amelia didn't need much persuasion to continue the story and carried on: "They arrived mid-morning, and Patrick was the most astonished of them all—the frigate was gone. It had disappeared without a trace.

Patrick stood motionless, his pulse quickening. He had seen it. He had boarded it. And now, it was as if it had never existed.

'But how could it just vanish like that? It wasn't seaworthy! It was right here!' He pointed at the empty shoreline, his voice laced with disbelief.

He pulled out his spyglass, scanning the coastline, then the horizon to the south, north, and east. Nothing. Just the relentless waves and the distant cry of seabirds. For a fleeting moment, he thought he caught a glimpse of sails barely visible in the mist—perhaps the same ship he had spotted the day before. But it was too far to tell.

'Maybe when the tide came in, the wind dragged it back out to sea,' Alexander Bauer suggested.

Patrick's heart sank. If that were true, the wreck—and his claim—were gone forever. Worse, he had dragged everyone out there for nothing. The *gauchos* who had come along exchanged skeptical glances. A stranded ship didn't just disappear overnight.

'It was right here,' Patrick insisted, gesturing broadly. 'It was huge—at least forty meters long, a proper frigate!'

One of the ranch hands, Antonio *"Antook"* Rivero, patted his shoulder. 'We believe you, don't worry. We'll follow the coast, see if it drifted. If it's out there, we'll find it.'

They split into two groups—one heading north for several kilometers, the other south toward Volunteer Point, circling back to *Puerto Soledad* along Berkeley Sound. But the ship was nowhere to be found. It had simply vanished—along with Patrick's dreams. That evening, Patrick went to see Annadee. She answered the door holding a lantern, her expression a mix of amusement and mischief. Word of his misadventure had already reached her.

'Hello, Patrick. What a lovely ship you have.'

Patrick sighed. 'Good evening, Annadee. So, you'll be teasing me too?'

She smirked. Of course. But tell me—was it a ghost ship? Or did it have headless sailors?'

'Hey, come here.' He took her hand, casting a quick glance to ensure her parents weren't near before kissing her. 'No ghosts. No headless sailors. Just a ship. And the tide must have taken it, or maybe it was still seaworthy enough to drift. But listen... I have proof.'

Annadee crossed her arms, raising a skeptical brow. 'Oh? Proof of what, Patrick?'

He hesitated. He didn't know what to do with the gold. He didn't want to lose it. He didn't even know if it was truly his to keep. But he also didn't want to get Annadee's hopes up for nothing.

'I found a chest on the ship. It had the name *Liberty Rose* engraved on it. I figure that must be the name of the frigate.'

Annadee tilted her head. '*Liberty Rose*? Never heard of it. And I've never seen a ship by that name in this port.'

She studied him for a moment, then grinned. 'Come on, admit it. You made it all up. Or maybe you fell asleep in the fields and dreamed of a shipwreck. That would be more believable.'

Patrick groaned. 'No, that's not it! I swear, I found a chest with the name on it.'

'Alright then, I suppose I believe you. So where is it? Where's this 'proof' of yours?'

Patrick hesitated. 'I hid it.'

Annadee rolled her eyes. 'And why, exactly, did you hide it? How am I supposed to believe you if I can't even see it?'

Patrick chuckled nervously. 'Well... if I tell you what was inside, you'll believe me even less.'

Annadee smirked. 'Let me guess—you found a treasure. Gold, silver, maybe precious stones?'

Patrick shifted uncomfortably. 'Actually... yes.'

Annadee's smile faded. She stared at him, unimpressed. 'Patrick Sans McGowan, who do you think I am? Stop this nonsense. If this is some game, I'm telling you—it's not working.'

Patrick sighed. 'I know how it sounds.'

'No, you don't! First, you 'find' a ship. Then, it disappears. Now, you claim you have a chest full of gold—but conveniently, you don't have it with you. And I'm supposed to believe this?'

'Shhh, keep your voice down, Annadee,' Patrick hushed, glancing around. 'Look, here's the deal: tomorrow afternoon, after I finish my tasks, I'll saddle your horse, and we'll go together. You'll see it with your own eyes. Then you'll know I'm telling the truth.'

Annadee hesitated, studying his face. Patrick wasn't one to lie—or joke about something this serious.

'Wait... you're serious?' She frowned. 'Hmm. Something tells me this is just an excuse to spend time with me.'

Patrick grinned. 'Well, it does sound that way, doesn't it? But honestly, you know how much I enjoy your company.'

He then told her everything—what he had seen on the coast, what he had found aboard the ship. However, he didn't reveal where he had hidden the chest. Not yet. Not until he knew what to do. He made her promise not to tell anyone until they figured it out together.

What neither of them knew was that forces beyond their control were already at play.

In the past few months, tensions in *Puerto Soledad* had escalated. The confiscation of the schooner *Harriet* in late July, the *Breakwater* in August, and the brigantine *Superior* had stirred unrest.

When the schooner *Breakwater* successfully escaped and its sailors returned to their home port in Stonington, Connecticut, they wasted no time in reporting to their government what was unfolding in the Falklands.

The response was swift.

Something was coming.

And perhaps, the ship Patrick had seen lingering near the bay wasn't bringing good news after all.

The following day, before Patrick and Annadee could retrieve the chest, the American corvette *USS Lexington* was spotted entering Berkeley Sound. Commanded by Master Commandant Silas Duncan, the ship raised a French flag, deceiving the residents of *Puerto Soledad*. No one grew concerned, nor did they suspect that enforcing the new laws over these islands might result in an attack—regardless of who might carry it out. Yet, this seemed to be precisely what was about to happen.

The *USS Lexington* reached *Puerto Soledad* on December 28, 1831, delayed by storms at the bay's entrance. Upon anchoring, a lieutenant and several men went ashore. They approached Captain Matthew Brisbane and Mr. Henry Metcalf, who were walking along the beach, and invited them aboard the *USS Lexington*. Once there, both men—being the highest-ranking authorities on the islands in Luis Vernet's absence—were immediately arrested.

In fact, Captain Davidson, who had been taken to Buenos Aires aboard the *Harriet* by Luis Vernet for trial, escaped as soon as he arrived in the city and had now returned to the Falkland Islands aboard the *USS Lexington*. Captain Davidson was well aware of who, besides Vernet, had been responsible for the confiscation of American ships and their belongings.

Following the arrests, another group of men disembarked in *Puerto Soledad* and unleashed their wrath upon the town, destroying almost everything in their path. Commander Silas Duncan of the *USS Lexington* was outraged by Vernet's accusations of piracy. Americans had long hunted and fished in the islands without issue, and, it was said, restrictions were only being imposed on the Americans, while the English faced no such prohibitions. Commander Duncan also claimed that Vernet had taken one of the seized ships for personal use, using it to transport his family to Buenos Aires. This made it evident that his actions were improper. Acts of piracy were punishable by hanging, and as such, the commander decided to destroy the port and recover everything confiscated from the three American ships.

The men disabled the cannons by spiking them, blew up the gunpowder, and destroyed firearms before throwing them into the bay. They razed houses, trampled vegetable gardens, confiscated pelts, and arrested more of Vernet's employees along with some townspeople. Many settlers fled into the fields upon witnessing the destruction, some not returning until after the *USS Lexington* had departed.

Although the Bauers and Patrick lived farther from the port, they soon learned of what had occurred. Several townsfolk fleeing to the countryside passed by and recounted the events. In some ways, the Bauers and Patrick were relieved, as they had no involvement in the confiscation of the American ships or Vernet's actions. They focused solely on their land and had no part in the governance of the town or the administration of the port.

With all this chaos unfolding in *Puerto Soledad*, Patrick's planned outing with Annadee to retrieve the chest was canceled. They couldn't risk going anywhere at that moment. Patrick also realized that because of these events, he could neither speak of his chest nor the *Liberty Rose*. If word got out, his treasure would likely be confiscated or stolen. He didn't bring the topic up again with Annadee. Although he had already shared everything with her, he wasn't sure she had believed him. It was better to wait for a more opportune moment to prove he was telling the truth. Moreover, with that small fortune, he could propose to her, buy land from Vernet upon his return, and start his own ranch. Everything would be fine—there was no need to worry.

During the *USS Lexington's* stay in port, Commander Duncan held a brief trial for the arrested men, assisted other ships, and even granted them free authorization to hunt and fish. Rumors were also spread about possible reprisals from American whalers and hunters against the remaining colony. In a way, Commander Duncan and Captain Davidson encouraged everyone to leave the islands. They also claimed that the government in Buenos Aires had disapproved of the confiscation of the American ships and that Vernet would not be returning.

This turned out to be true. Luis Vernet and his family never returned to the Falkland Islands. As a result, many decided to abandon their homes and leave the islands entirely.

Alexander and Marie Anne, Annadee's parents, were no strangers to the growing unease. They wanted to stay. After all, they had invested over two years of their lives in this new colony—a considerable time—but circumstances had changed. If the rumors were true, the assaults and robberies would continue. And while life in *Banda Oriental* might not be much better, it was now an independent country with an established constitution.

On January 20, 1832, Alexander Bauer went to the port to request passage from Commander Duncan aboard his ship. He was ready to return to Montevideo. Two other German families also chose to leave, bringing the total to thirty-two settlers. With everything destroyed and no authority or means to defend against future attacks, this was no longer the place they had dreamed of building a life. It wasn't a place for their daughter, either. The suspicion that Luis Vernet would never return only cemented their decision.

The next day, with all work suspended, the Bauer Fischers and Patrick gathered for lunch. There was much to discuss and plan. They wanted to ensure that whatever they decided, it was fair and right. Alexander extended an invitation to Patrick to leave with them. It was the most logical choice, knowing how deeply his daughter loved Patrick and how fond both he and Marie Anne were of him. But Patrick wasn't so sure. When he met Annadee and left the *Elbe*, he had committed to staying. He dreamed of raising a family on these islands. Another drastic change wasn't what he wanted. Besides, he didn't believe the colony was doomed. Many settlers planned to stay despite the threats from the Americans. And returning to Montevideo? How would he bring back the gold he had found?

'Patrick, son, be reasonable,' Alexander urged. 'Have you seen what's left of *Puerto Soledad*? Do you think this won't happen again? There's no authority, no soldiers, no weapons. Nearly everything has been destroyed. Thankfully, no lives were lost. But you know Annadee won't stay here, don't you? What will you say to her, Patrick?'

'Has she told you she won't stay?' Patrick countered, though he knew she wouldn't disobey her parents. 'Have you even asked her?'

'There's no need to ask. She won't stay here, in this... place—if we can still call it that. There's nothing left, Patrick. It's over. Do you understand? This isn't the only place to start over. We're not even from the Malvinas. If we managed to emigrate here, we can do it again. What happens when other whalers and hunters hear about this? What if they come back and steal again? All our hard work—gone. You're young... both of you are young, with your whole lives ahead of you. But here? I don't know what kind of future you could have. There needs to be structure—government, authority, respect, stability—and none of that exists here. What happened will bring more problems, politically and locally. This could spark a war between Spain, the United Provinces, the United States, and England. You've heard of the English claims to these islands, haven't you? Take my advice. Come with us. Annadee would be happy with you anywhere, but this is not the place or the time to build a family.' Alexander's voice grew firm as he punctuated his words with a decisive thump on the table, rattling the dishes and casting a heavy silence over the room.

Annadee and her mother, busy in the kitchen, rushed in, alarmed by the sudden noise. For a moment, they thought the Americans had returned.

'What happened? What was that noise?' Marie Anne asked. 'Is everything all right?'

'Yes, everything's fine. I accidentally knocked the candlestick off the table,' Alexander replied, his gaze fixed on Patrick. He wasn't ready to explain the real reason to the women. He didn't want to worry his daughter more than necessary. If Patrick refused to come with them, he knew Annadee's heart would break. He also knew that, if it came to it, he would force her to leave rather than let her endure the hardships he feared were coming.

Annadee glanced at Patrick, sensing the tension in the room. He avoided her gaze. Something wasn't right.

By Sunday, January 22, the *USS Lexington* was ready to set sail.

Patrick, still undecided and not convinced about leaving, begged Annadee to stay. He told her everything would be fine, and they could rebuild the port, the town, and the fields.

'Patrick, don't put me in this impossible position. You know I love you, but I think my parents are right. I don't want to disobey them—I'm their only daughter. Do you think they would leave if I stayed? And I don't want to force them to stay either. If something were to happen to them, I couldn't live with myself. Please understand me, I beg you. We can start over somewhere else; what does *Islas Malvinas* matter? Let's go back to Montevideo. Despite what I told you that day on the beach, everything that's happened has crushed my dreams of staying here. Please, let's go. Everything we can take is packed in trunks already. Father says that when we arrive in Montevideo, he'll go to Buenos Aires to speak with *Don* Vernet to recover his investment. Everything will turn out fine. Trust me, please.'

They both knew time was running out. The ship would depart on schedule, waiting for no one. The Americans were eager to take the prisoners to trial—it had already been nearly a month since their capture and detention on the islands.

For Patrick, the thought of staying alone on the island without Annadee was unbearable. Yet if he left, he couldn't abandon the chest. That chest held his future.

'All right, all right, Annadee. You're right,' Patrick finally relented, his voice quiet but filled with something she couldn't quite name—hesitation? Resolve?

'Let's do this. But I need to retrieve the chest— it's not far. I'll be back in about two hours. There's still plenty of time before the ship departs.'

Annadee's breath caught, her heart pounding. 'Really? You mean it?' she whispered, clutching his hands as though afraid he'd slip away if she let go.

He nodded, and relief burst through her like sunlight after a storm.

'I knew you wouldn't let me go alone!' she exclaimed, throwing her arms around him. 'I was so afraid, Patrick—so afraid you wouldn't come.'

He cupped her face for a brief second, then pulled away. 'I have to go.'

'Then I'm coming with you.'

He tensed. 'No, Annadee.' His grip on her arms tightened. 'It's better if I go alone. Help your parents, and don't say a word to anyone. If people find out, I don't know what they might do. Just as they looted the port, they'd do the same to me. Who knows if it wasn't them who attacked the *Liberty Rose*? No one must know. I'll hide the chest among my things when I board.'

She hesitated. Something about his words, his tone, sent a chill through her.

But she forced herself to nod. 'Yes, Patrick. I won't say anything. I love you!'

'And I love you too, Annadee.'

She kissed him, her fingers knotting into his jacket, as if she could anchor him to her, hold him here, safe. But then, too soon, he pulled away, mounted his dapple gray horse, *Oriental*, and rode off into the growing mist.

She stood there, breathless, watching him disappear beyond the hills.

And then… she waited.

The hours dragged on, each moment an eternity. The dock bustled with sailors, passengers, and the final calls of departure. But Patrick did not return.

Annadee's hands trembled as she checked the sun's position. Not yet. He still has time.

Then—a gust of wind. The ship's sails unfurled.

Her stomach dropped.

'No. No, no, not yet—please, not yet!'

She ran to Commander Duncan, pleading, 'A little longer! Please! He's coming, I swear!'

The man shook his head. 'Miss, we can't wait any longer. Is getting dark. We must sail now'

Her father's voice cut through the air, sharp as a blade. 'He's not coming back, Annadee.'

'He is!' she shot back, chest heaving. 'You don't know that!'

Her mother's eyes brimmed with sorrow. 'If he meant to leave with you, he would be here.'

Annadee's breath hitched, her pulse hammering against her ribs. 'Something happened to him. He wouldn't just—'

'He made his choice.' Alexander's voice was like stone. 'Face it. He stayed.'

Desperate, Annadee wanted to get off the ship to wait or search for him, but her parents refused to let her. Their trust in Patrick had vanished. They suspected his last-minute trip to the countryside was merely an excuse to avoid leaving with them—or facing a proper farewell. That's when Annadee broke her silence and told them what Patrick had gone to retrieve, but they didn't believe him. Alexander, recalling his argument with Patrick the night before, was convinced that he had chosen to stay.

The words punched the air from her lungs.

'Patrick—her Patrick—chose to stay?'

'No.'

No, that wasn't true.

Something had delayed him. He was out there, riding hard, racing back to her—he had to be.

She turned to the shore, scouring the horizon, eyes burning, scanning every road, every hill, praying, pleading—*where are you, Patrick?*

Nothing.

Then—the ship lurched.

The anchor lifted. The crew shouted orders.

They were leaving.

Annadee's heart slammed against her ribs. She whirled around, panic clawing at her throat. 'No! I can't leave—I have to find him!'

Her father's grip locked around her arm. 'Enough.'

She struggled, gasping, twisting away. 'Let me go!'

Her mother clutched her, voice trembling. 'Annadee, stop! We have to go!'

Annadee sobbed, her knees threatening to buckle as the ship pulled away from the dock, away from the land—away from Patrick.

She gripped the railing with white-knuckled hands, desperate, eyes locked on the fading coastline. She searched and searched, her lips moving in frantic whispers.

Please, Patrick. Please, my love, come back to me...

But he never did.

The bay grew distant, the hills softened, the land became a mere shadow against the horizon.

And then—it was gone.

She let out a broken, keening sob, her body trembling. Her mother wrapped her in a trembling embrace, but Annadee barely felt it.

Her father's words echoed in her mind, brutal and final.

'He made his choice.'

No.

Something had happened.

Had he been delayed? Had someone stopped him? Had he changed his mind? The questions burned through her, an agony she could barely endure.

And then, slowly… the guilt crept in.

Had she abandoned him? Had she left too soon? If she had fought harder, stayed longer, would he have made it?

She pressed a shaking hand to her stomach.

Patrick didn't know.

She hadn't told him.

She might be carrying his child.

A choked sob escaped her lips as realization crashed over her.

She had left. And now, she might never know what happened to him.

She might never see him again.

And the love of her life was lost to her forever.

The only hope keeping her going was the thought that he might return to Uruguay later, taking the next available ship. That's what her mother said to calm her. If their love was real, he would follow her, boarding the first ship bound for Montevideo.

But time passed, and that never happened. He never came looking for her, and no one ever heard from him again. She wrote him letters whenever she could, sending them on every ship traveling to the Falkland Islands, but they were never answered."

Chapter XVII

Return to the Islands

"Annadee never married. After her parents passed away in Uruguay in 1847, she decided to return to the Falkland Islands with her daughter. By then, Patricia was about fifteen years old.

On their return journey, as the beloved San Luis Peninsula appeared on the horizon, Annadee stood at the bow with her daughter, unable to take her eyes off the coastline. The salty wind tangled in her hair, carrying with it the distant cries of seabirds and the scent of home. Memories of Patrick flooded her mind—his laughter, the warmth of his embrace, the way his eyes held unspoken promises. She imagined him still waiting for her, riding *Oriental*, his beloved horse, along the shoreline or atop a windswept cliff, scanning the horizon as he had always done. Her heart ached with longing, even as she knew deep down that he would not be there.

After settling in Port Stanley, she wandered the familiar landscapes of her youth, revisiting every place they had shared. She walked the winding paths where their footsteps had once mingled, traced the edges of the cliffs where they had stood side by side, and sat for hours on the beaches where they had whispered dreams of the future. But Patrick was nowhere to be found.

Some claimed he had left on a ship long ago, vanishing into the vastness of the sea. Others insisted he had never passed through the village at all, as if he had been nothing more than a ghost in her memory. But Annadee refused to believe that he had simply disappeared without a trace. Every face in the crowd, every shadow at dusk, every whisper of the wind carried the cruel hope that, somehow, he was still out there.

And so, she searched—for days, for weeks, for years. But no matter how many times she retraced their steps, Patrick remained lost to time, leaving only echoes of a love that had never truly been given the chance to unfold.

Antonina Roxa, Annadee's friend who had remained on the islands, returned all the letters Annadee had sent over the years. Not a single one had ever been collected. The ink had faded, the paper worn with time, yet they remained unread—messages lost to the void.

Each time a new ship docked in Stanley, Annadee asked about Patrick. She searched the faces of strangers, hoping for news, for a whisper of his fate. But the answer was always the same: silence.

And so, the years slipped away. Annadee never learned what became of Patrick, and the mystery of his disappearance lingered in her heart until the very end."

"That's how it was," Amelia finished softly, her voice carrying the weight of sorrow.

"What a sad story, Grandma," Nina murmured, her young eyes clouded with emotion.

"Yes, Nina. Very sad. Annadee must have suffered deeply for Patrick."

"But…" Víctor interjected, his brow furrowed in disbelief, "did they search all the islands? Didn't they ask those who stayed behind? How could someone who loved these islands—and Annadee—so much just vanish? And why didn't he go to Montevideo to find her?"

Amelia sighed, her gaze distant, as if peering into the past. "We don't know, Mr. Cabot. What we do know is that they searched for him—she searched for him—until the day she died. Annadee never gave up hope that, one day, he would return from some distant place to find her.

Her final words before she passed were: 'Now I will go to the only place I have not searched, and if he is there, I will be with him for all eternity.'

Annadee died in 1888, at the age of seventy-six."

A heavy silence filled the room.

"Poor Annadee," Víctor murmured, shaking his head. "Now I understand. I can only imagine the desperation she must have felt back then. Travel was slow, communication was nearly impossible, and letters could take weeks, months… or never arrive at all."

He exhaled, his voice tinged with quiet reverence. "That must be why she returned—to find peace, somehow. Do you know what happened to the letters Annadee sent to Patrick? And her diary?"

"Yes, of course," Amelia replied. "I've kept everything. I've read her letters and diary many times. That's how I know all that happened—how deeply she felt and how much she suffered. It's a treasured family relic now."

"It's heartbreaking," Diana added. "Like being left at the altar. Why would he do that to her?"

"I don't know," Amelia sighed. "Maybe he feared losing his fortune. If the treasure was real, perhaps he was afraid someone would take it from him, just like the confiscated goods. Maybe his love for gold outweighed his love for Annadee. Or maybe he didn't want to return to Montevideo and face his father—I don't know. But from her letters, I can tell how much she suffered. I've cried more than once reading them. She never understood why he left—or where he went. Yet, in the end, she forgave him. She wrote it in her journal and in several letters. I'm not sure I would have."

"And what about the treasure?" Víctor asked. "Did anyone ever search for it? Was it ever found?"

"Where would they search?" Amelia replied. "First, we don't even know if it truly existed. And second, so much time has passed. If there was treasure, someone else might have searched for it by now. But at least no one in our family ever did."

"Tell me, I know I may be intruding on family matters, but... could I read those letters?"

Amelia snapped out of her thoughts, caught off guard by the question. Her voice was firm as she replied, "No one outside our family has ever read them. Few even know they exist, and that's how it will stay. Those letters... they were meant for Patrick. They're intimate, personal. A treasure passed down through generations. I don't think anyone could truly understand or respect her feelings the way we do."

Víctor nodded, absorbing the weight of her words. "Of course... I understand. I didn't mean to make you uncomfortable."

"Mom, please! It's been so long. Maybe it's time to move on."

Amelia sighed. "Ashley, I know. But you know me. It's not that simple. Maybe I'm a fool, but I just… I can't let go."

"Mrs. Amelia, you don't need to apologize," Víctor said gently. "I respect that completely. These are family matters, and I understand. Again, I'm sorry."

Her expression softened. "It's alright. I understand your position as a journalist." She hesitated for a moment before adding, "But believe me when I say—she suffered. A lot."

Víctor felt a pang of regret. While he wished he could read the letters, he knew better than to push further. Amelia had clearly taken this all to heart, suffering in ways that echoed Annadee's pain. So, he said nothing more. Deep down, he also felt that she hadn't left out anything important.

"But would it be possible to visit Port Louis and explore the place? Could you get permission from the owners for me?" Víctor asked.

"Of course," Paul replied. "The owner is my brother-in-law, Amelia's brother, David Ferguson. I'll give him a call later."

"That's a surprising coincidence. Thank you so much." Víctor said.

Then Amelia added, "But I'll tell you this, Mr. Cabot—don't hold Patrick in high regard for the story you're writing. He was nothing more than a man who played with someone's feelings, someone who loved him deeply, and, unknowingly, left a daughter without a father."

Víctor nodded, understanding her feelings. "Yes, of course."

"Alright," Amelia continued. "So, what exactly are you hoping to see in Port Louis?"

"I've read about the colony's origins and the old capital. It would be invaluable for me to see the area in person. I want to write a story as close to reality as possible, and visiting the place will make that easier."

"I understand. No problem. I'll mention that when I call. You're staying until Thursday, right?"

"That's right," Diana answered. "We're leaving Thursday afternoon. I have things to do on Friday, so we won't stay any longer."

Víctor turned to Paul. "I really want to thank you for your hospitality and kindness in welcoming us into your home. I have to say, your place is fantastic. It has a certain magic to it."

Paul chuckled. "Well, come live in the Falklands. You'll see you're making good friends here," he said, turning to Diana. "You're happy here, aren't you, Diana?"

"Yes, that's true," she replied.

"Honestly, it's better than I imagined," Víctor said, smiling. "Thank you again for the invitation. I'll keep it in mind."

"You haven't seen the snowstorms and fierce winds yet," Paul said with a grin. "But those have their own charm too." He stood up, excusing himself to make the call to David Ferguson.

Víctor watched him leave and wondered about the treasure. Who would it belong to if they found it? Would it be Patrick's family, the landowners, or the person who found it? Or perhaps all three? He'd already gained so much: the story, new friendships, travel, and an adventure in the Falkland Islands—something he never would have imagined. Still, his curiosity about the treasure lingered.

Paul returned, sitting next to Víctor. "I spoke with them. There's no problem. We're going tomorrow."

"Perfect!" Víctor replied. "Thank you."

"Yes, great," Diana added, "And luckily, the weather will be nice tomorrow. No rain or snow in the forecast for the rest of the week."

"Couldn't be better," Víctor said, his tone full of anticipation.

Chapter XVIII

Port Louis and Mount Twelve O'Clock

It was still dark when Víctor woke up to the sound of voices in the kitchen. He looked at the clock and realized it was later than what he had thought. He quickly remembered that in this part of the world, the sun doesn't rise very early. The wind had died down considerably, and the whistling sound from the window was gone, unlike the night before. This reassured him. He got up, hurriedly dressed, and went to the kitchen, where everyone was already gathered—including Nina. A bit embarrassed, he apologized for waking up late, saying that the bed was too comfortable, and it made him want to stay there.

"I'm glad you slept well. And don't worry, Víctor, it's not late at all. It's just that the sun takes its time around here," Paul replied.

"Very well then. So, who else is going to Port Louis today?" he asked eagerly.

"We're going to take advantage of visiting my brother, so we're all going," Amelia said. "It will be a family gathering."

"Excellent. Once we get there, I'll show you something I think you'll find very interesting."

"Oh, well... what is it? What's it about?"

"It's related to my research. I think your brother will find it fascinating too."

"Oh, yes! Of course, we want to know what you've researched."

They finished breakfast and left.

Upon arriving in Port Louis, Víctor felt more at ease. Finally, he was standing in the very place where it all happened. He was closer than ever to solving the mystery.

The scenery was breathtaking—like something out of a Thomas Cole painting. Aside from the modern buildings, the place seemed largely unchanged since it was established as the capital of the Falkland Islands. At that moment, he partly understood why the French had chosen this place to establish the first settlement on the islands in 1764.

Port Louis consisted of about eight houses, one huge shearing shed, three smaller sheds, and a dock, some greenhouses, somewhat dispersed. From the entrance to this place, one could spot the cemetery and the ruins of the old fort. Now Víctor could clearly imagine how the place had looked at the beginning of the colony, when Patrick and Annadee had arrived many years ago.

David and Caroline, the estate owners, came out to greet them. After introducing themselves and exchanging greetings with the rest of the family, they invited them inside.

Once inside the living room, Caroline offered tea or coffee.

"Thank you, but we're fine. We had breakfast before leaving," Amelia replied.

Víctor also thanked her and then commented on the estate, "You have a beautiful place. I saw it in photos online. Obviously, it's very different in person. I can see that not much remains of the old capital, right?"

"No, but there's still something," David said. "The original cemetery is still there, along with some ruins of the fortifications and parts of Luis Vernet's house. There are also other foundations, but they're almost gone now. I'll show you later, if you like."

"Of course, I think it would be very interesting to see them, thank you. Besides, that was one of the reasons for coming," Víctor replied.

"You've had quite a journey to get here. I hope everything's going well for you. Paul told me you're writing about Annadee and Patrick," Caroline said.

"Yes, that's right, Caroline. An article for a newspaper—maybe even a book," Víctor replied.

"How interesting," Caroline said thoughtfully. "David and I were wondering why you chose them. It's not a well-known or particularly significant story. What exactly do you plan to write about, if you don't mind me asking?"

"On the contrary, I'm glad you asked," Víctor said with a smile. "And you're right—it's not a well-known story. But, as I told your family, this story chose me, not the other way around. During my research, I stumbled upon something intriguing, and I think it's worth investigating further."

"Oh, really? What did you find, Víctor?" David asked, leaning in with interest.

"Yes," Amelia added, "you've kept us intrigued since breakfast. I hope you'll finally tell us now that we're all here."

Víctor nodded. "Well, I think it's time to share the story I discovered by accident."

"This sounds interesting," Caroline said. "Professor McIntyre came to Port Louis a couple of times to investigate Patrick's life, but he never found anything important."

"That's true," David agreed.

"I know," Víctor replied. "He mentioned that when I arrived. Honestly, when I left Uruguay for the Falkland Islands, I had no idea there were any living relatives of Annadee or Patrick here. It was a surprise to find Annadee's grave—and her daughter Patricia's—in the Stanley cemetery. Even more surprising was seeing that someone still remembers her, leaving flowers on the anniversary of her passing."

"Yes," Amelia said softly. "We're the only descendants. Perhaps that's why it's easier to keep the story alive."

Víctor nodded. "It was a coincidence that I arrived on the anniversary of her death."

Ashley chimed in, "I was the one who left the flowers. We go every year."

"I see," Víctor said. "Anyway, now that we're all here, I want to show you something and tell you what I found."

"Alright, what's it about?" Amelia asked, curiosity in her eyes. "Do you know something else about him? Did you find his grave in Uruguay?"

"No, none of that," Víctor replied. "I don't know where his grave is, if it even exists. He was a sailor; he could have died anywhere in the world. But I believe there's something of his still on this island."

"Oh… But why do you think that?" Amelia asked.

Víctor leaned forward. "The story I've been following is more complex than you imagine. Let me tell you how it all started: A few weeks ago, I got an assignment from the newspaper in my city. I had to photograph some fishing boats at the Paysandú shipyard that were ready to be scrapped. That's where I found the remains of the *Fennia*."

Diana's eyes widened in surprise. "The same *Fennia* that was in Stanley? The one we talked about at dinner the other night?"

"Yes, the very same," Víctor confirmed. "I didn't want to say anything then, but I already knew of its existence."

"The *Fennia*?" Paul asked.

"Yes, that ship ended up in my city. It was dismantled there in 1977."

"I remember that ship," Paul said. "It was in Stanley Harbor when I was a kid. Do you remember it? The four-masted sailing ship?"

"I do," David affirmed.

"And so do I," Amelia added. "But I never knew what happened to it. I thought it had been sent to the U.S. as a museum."

"No, Amelia, it never made it," Víctor explained. "The company ran out of money, leaving the Fennia abandoned in Montevideo's port. After years of neglect, it was eventually taken to Paysandú for scrapping."

Amelia frowned. "And what does that have to do with Annadee and Patrick? That ship didn't even exist when they were alive."

"Exactly," Víctor said, leaning forward. "That's what caught my attention when I made my discovery."

Caroline tilted her head. "Well, you've got us intrigued, Mr. Cabot. What's the connection between the *Fennia* and them? What did you find?"

"Alright, I'll keep it short," Víctor said. "When the *Fennia* was scrapped in 1977, a small box was found in the hold. It was assumed to have belonged to the ship's doctor and was considered unimportant. Inside was a letter, but it was in another language, and no one knew what it said. Forty years later, I happened to meet the man who found it. He gave me the box so I could translate the letter and figure out what it was. That was what led me here."

"Okay, but what did the letter say?" Diana asked. "Who wrote it?"

Víctor took a deep breath. "It was from a German prisoner named Karl Henning. At first, I thought it was just an old letter with no real significance. But then something caught my attention. Henning wrote that he and Sergeant Hans Schneider survived the sinking of their ship in 1939 but were taken prisoner. He didn't give many more details. Now, the question is—why was that letter in that box? And how did that box end up on the *Fennia*?"

"And?" Diana pressed. "Did you find anything else?"

Víctor nodded. "Examining the box more closely, I discovered a hidden compartment—very well concealed. Inside, there was another document."

"Another letter?"

"No," Víctor said, his voice steady. "It was something else. A map. With geographical annotations."

"A map of what?" Amelia asked, her eyes narrowing.

"At first, I wasn't completely sure. That's why I'm here," Víctor admitted. "But on that map, there was a faint marking—almost invisible—shaped like an X. And two names."

He let the silence hang for a moment before finishing.

"One was Patrick's. The other was Liberty Rose."

"Our Patrick?" Ashley asked, her voice barely above a whisper.

"That's right," Víctor confirmed. "While searching for information, I discovered who he was. That's when I learned he disappeared here."

Amelia shook her head. "I don't understand, Víctor. How could a letter from 1939 mention him?"

"Exactly," Víctor said. "That's what puzzled me. How could someone who vanished in 1832 be referenced on a 1939 map? And how did they know about the *Liberty Rose*—a ghost ship, until last Monday."

"Wait... what do you mean, 'until last Monday'?" Amelia asked, clearly surprised.

"That's another surprise I have for you."

"Well, you're full of surprises, Víctor," she added.

"And here's where things get even stranger. According to Professor McIntyre, just last Saturday, a fishing boat recovered some lanterns near the entrance of Berkeley Sound. They had *Liberty Rose* engraved on them. The professor is studying them at the museum right now. Since leaving Uruguay, I've had this hunch—there's something about Patrick and the *Liberty Rose* hidden near here."

"That can't be. I'm more confused than ever," Amelia said, bewildered.

"And so am I," added Caroline.

"Karl Henning and Hans Schneider were on this island before they were taken prisoner. Somehow, they came across something from Patrick and the *Liberty Rose*."

"Did you bring the map? Can we see it?" they all asked at once.

"Yes, of course."

Víctor retrieved the small box from the *Fennia* out of his backpack, carefully dismantling it as he had the first time. As he unfolded the map, everyone leaned in.

After a moment, David said, "This doesn't seem right. I know these coasts well. This map doesn't look like it's from around here."

"I thought the same at first," Víctor replied. "It's a strange map, almost like it was drawn from memory. The compass is reversed—what appears to be north is actually south. I've checked every island in the area, and this is the only place that fits."

"There are countless bays and hills here—or anywhere in the world," David argued. "This could all be a coincidence, Mr. Cabot."

"David, I understand. But if we're here, the only way to know is to check the spot marked with the X," Víctor insisted.

"Where's the mark?" Paul asked.

Víctor pointed to the center of the map, between what seemed to be three hills.

"Hmm, I can't see it clearly," David said.

Víctor rummaged through his backpack, pulled out the photocopy with clearer markings, and laid it on the table. Everyone studied it intently.

"What do you think, David?" Paul asked.

David sighed. "It seems to be near Twelve O'Clock Hill. I've been there dozens of times—nothing but rocks. Are you sure?"

Víctor glanced at the map, then at Diana. He wanted to say yes, but the truth weighed on him.

"No," he admitted softly. "It's just a theory— pieces of a puzzle I've gathered. The only way to confirm it is to go up there."

He opened his notebook, laying out all his notes. "This is everything I have. If I'm right, we'll find something at the summit. If not, well, at least I tried."

Amelia looked at David, her voice tinged with anxiety. "So, what do we do?"

"Wait," Víctor interjected. "Think it through. I have a hand-drawn map from someone who was on these islands and later on the *Fennia*. It bears Patrick's name and the *Liberty Rose*. That's too many coincidences to ignore."

They exchanged uncertain glances, torn between doubt and hope.

"Wait! I almost forgot," Víctor exclaimed. "I found another letter yesterday—from Hans Schneider. It corroborates Karl's story." He pulled out his camera and showed them a photo of the letter. "This proves it."

David exhaled deeply. "Alright... the map doesn't quite match, but your evidence is compelling. It's nearby. We can go."

He paused, then added, "I'll help you. You're not going alone. It's not the best time of year to be up there, but I'll go with you. What does everyone else think?"

"Well, yes, I think it's worth it," Amelia said. Paul and Ashley nodded in agreement.

"And I want to know what's up there, too," Caroline said. "With everything you've told us, I think we should try. We can't just leave it unanswered."

"Thank you! And of course, I'm glad to have your help! Honestly, I wouldn't be able to do this any other way," Víctor exclaimed, excitedly. "Shall we go right now?"

David laughed.

"My, how impatient you are, Mr. Cabot! What's the rush? Do you think whatever's up there is going to get up and leave? Besides, we should bring some tools—at least a shovel, a pickaxe. Don't you think? How do you plan on finding it? If there's anything up there, it's hidden underground or among the rocks. Better if we prepare, eat lunch, and head out afterward. Agreed?"

"Of course, David. You're right. I guess I'm just a bit impatient," Víctor admitted, trying to compose himself.

David invited Víctor to accompany him to the shed to gather tools. Later, he would take them on a tour to see the ruins of old Port Louis.

After lunch, Amelia decided to stay behind with Nina and Caroline, while the others got into the Rovers and set off.

The drive to the summit area took about twenty minutes. The rest of the climb would have to be done on foot. They carried tools on their shoulders—shovel, pickaxe, a long crowbar, and a flashlight—and made their way up. The wind remained calm, though occasional stronger gusts blew through. Despite the sunshine, the air stayed very cold. Four hours remained until sunset.

Plenty of time, thought Víctor. But when he reached the top, he realized the summit was much larger than he'd imagined. It stretched about a hundred meters long by thirty wide, with ten mounds standing out for their height and size. This meant there were multiple possible locations to search.

The view from up there was stunning. It was almost possible to see the entire peninsula, stretching all the way to the sea and the mouth of Berkeley Bay. From that height, Port Louis looked farther away than it had in Karl's sketch, but Víctor dismissed the discrepancy.

Once they arrived, they gathered behind one of the taller rocks for shelter from the constant wind and began to talk.

"As you can see, Mr. Cabot, this won't be as easy as you thought. There are countless places to search. Perhaps it would be better to bring in specialists or better tools, don't you think?" David asked.

"Now that I see it in person, you might be right," Víctor admitted.

"Besides, as I said before, I've never seen anything unusual up here."

"I think it's just a matter of searching," Víctor said, studying the map. "From what I gather and how I interpret the sketch, whatever we're looking for must be on the southwest side, facing the harbor." He pointed to the mark on the map.

"Alright then, let's start here and see how far we get," David suggested.

"Sounds good. Let's do it!" Víctor agreed enthusiastically.

Diana, Víctor, David, Paul, and Ashley formed a line, spaced about two meters apart, and began scanning the ground for any clues—special markings, anomalies among the rocks. The terrain was extremely rocky, and if something was buried there, it wouldn't be easy to find. Using the crowbar they'd brought, they struck any spots that seemed suspicious—ground, stones, crevices—listening for a different sound or looking for signs of something unusual.

After two hours, they realized that unless they found something soon, they wouldn't have enough daylight to cover the entire summit.

At first, Víctor had been brimming with excitement, convinced they'd uncover something that day. But as time dragged on with no results, his worry grew. He didn't want to seem like a fool in front of these people. After all, he had appeared out of nowhere with a story they hardly believed, so he needed to find something—anything—that indicated something significant had happened there.

When another two hours passed without any discovery, they decided to take a break and come up with a better plan. Víctor suggested focusing their search on the sides of the tallest rocks, which would narrow the possibilities by more than half. If they still found nothing, they could leave the rest for the next day.

Ashley, carrying a thermos of coffee, invited everyone to sit and relax for a moment. As they sipped their coffee, the group began voicing doubts about the likelihood of finding anything. Not wanting to hear their skepticism, Víctor wandered off a short distance, letting his gaze drift over the vast landscape as the scenery washed over him.

The view was breathtaking. He seized the moment—and the scenery—to take several photos. For a fleeting second, he wondered if he could ever call this place home. It was lonely, cold, and windswept—yet something about its raw beauty captivated him.

Víctor stood for a while, observing the brilliant blue sky dotted with wandering white clouds, the gray hues of the rocky mountains blending into brownish-green slopes below. The gorse bushes, with their yellow blossoms, added cheerful strokes of color. Sheep grazed lazily on the hillsides, and the grass, swaying gently in the wind like waves on an invisible sea lent a touch of life and motion to the scene. The reflection of the sky and clouds in the bay's waters completed the masterpiece.

When they finished their coffee, they noticed the temperature dropping quickly. The sun continued its steady march toward the horizon, casting longer shadows and gradually stealing its warmth. They wouldn't be able to keep searching much longer. It was six degrees Celsius, and soon it would drop below zero. The wind, though calm, was relentless, making their exposure to the elements even more challenging.

"You've been lucky, Víctor," Paul said as Víctor rejoined the group. "These past few days have been pretty mild for winter. Usually, it's cloudy, raining, snowing, and even colder than this. Next week's forecast is calling for all that—snow and freezing temperatures. If I'd known you were coming for this, I'd have suggested waiting until summer."

"You're absolutely right. The professor said the same thing. This isn't the best weather for this, but we'll push on anyway. Besides, I'm sure we'll find something any moment now. We must be close."

"I think you confused Uruguay's winters with this," Diana teased. "You didn't expect this much wind and cold, did you?"

"Not at all," Víctor replied. "Sometimes Uruguay's weather is similar, but we don't get nearly as much wind."

"Let's keep going," Paul said. "We've got about an hour left before we need to head back."

That hour passed quickly. They carefully examined the tallest stone mounds but found nothing—not even a marking. While they didn't discover any clues that day, they resolved to return the next day unless the weather worsened. There were still several promising spots left to check.

Before beginning the descent, they took a group photo to commemorate the effort. As the others started heading down, Víctor made a quick pass around two more sites, hoping to spot something obvious—but no luck. Disappointed and lost in thought, he began following the group down from a distance.

They reached Port Louis after dark. They stepped inside the house just long enough to say goodbye and organize their plans for the next day. Nina wasn't feeling well, so the Smiths wouldn't be coming along. It would be only David, Caroline, Diana, and Víctor continuing the search.

The following day would be decisive for Víctor since he didn't have much time left to keep looking.

Before saying goodbye to Víctor, David Ferguson looked at his wife as if asking for permission to speak, then turned to Víctor:

"Look, all of this is very interesting, but as I've said before, it doesn't seem like there's anything up there. I want—and I think we all want—your theory to be true, but I'm starting to think it's just that—a theory. This all happened so long ago. Maybe we should just let it rest."

"Yes, David," Víctor interrupted, "I understand. I've been asking myself if I'm right or..."

"But let me finish," David interjected. "Even so, we'll help you as much as we can. So go and get some rest now. We'll meet here early tomorrow. Okay?"

Víctor knew his journey would end that Sunday, and even if he wanted to extend it, getting Roberto González's approval or further assistance from the Smiths or the Fergusons was unlikely. On top of that, the weather was forecasted to worsen the following week with snow and freezing temperatures. If he didn't find something the next day, perhaps no one ever would. It was a thought that would haunt him for the rest of his life. His story would go nowhere, and he wouldn't have much to report back to Roberto. Nor could he afford another trip to the Falkland Islands if he wanted to continue his research. So much effort and enthusiasm for nothing. The thought left him uneasy. Time was his worst enemy.

The journey back to the Smiths' farm was a quiet one for Víctor. Lost in thought, he reflected on how he hadn't found anything and how nothing had gone as he imagined. He understood that the drawing might not match reality. After all, many years had passed. Still, for some reason, he felt like something was missing. His thoughts grew darker: What if all of this was Karl's invention? Could he have fabricated the drawing to bribe a guard and escape by promising a treasure map in return? Could he have heard about Patrick's disappearance and spun the story from there?

Noticing his concern, Diana broke the silence.

"What's wrong, Víctor? Did you think you were Indiana Jones? It's not like in the movies, is it? Why didn't you tell me all these details earlier?"

"Yes... I suppose I could have, but I wasn't sure... and, well, I'm still not. Besides, the *Fennia* kept this secret for so many years. Maybe there was a reason for that. The worst part is that maybe this is all made up, and there's nothing up there."

"Don't feel that way. At least you'll have a good story, and now you've met me too, right?" Diana said, laughing. "That's something, isn't it, Víctor?"

"Yeah, thanks, Diana. You're a treasure. I know it's been a beautiful adventure, a wonderful trip, and a great story. But I'll feel like an idiot if we don't find anything. And besides, I'm troubling these people... and you."

Ashley, who had been silent in the back with Nina sleeping on her lap, spoke up:

"Don't feel that way, Víctor. My parents understand perfectly. My uncle and aunt too. They're very excited about the possibility of finding something about Patrick. So don't worry about us. It's all fine."

"Thank you, Ashley. You have no idea how much it helps to hear that. Even so, I have to find something tomorrow."

At Isthmus Camp during dinner, Víctor thanked the Smiths for everything and apologized. Amelia assured him there was no need. If there was any chance of learning more about Patrick, it was worth the effort.

After a shower and before heading to bed, Víctor restlessly reviewed the letters and map again. Now that he'd been to the site and seen the summit of the hill, perhaps he could better understand Karl's drawings. He took out his camera and examined the photos he'd taken from up there. With those images, he imagined what he might have drawn if he were standing there in 1939.

When he finished, everyone else had gone to bed except Paul, who was in the kitchen when Víctor walked in.

"Hey, I thought you'd be asleep by now," Paul said, surprised.

"Well, no, Mister Smith. I've been going over the map again. Something doesn't add up, and it's been bothering me. Something isn't right."

"What exactly do you mean? What isn't right?"

"I've been studying the letters and map this whole time. It's possible Karl made all of this up for another purpose. If he learned about the mystery of Patrick and the *Liberty Rose*, he might have fabricated the entire story to bribe someone—a guard—to escape from *Fennia*. It could all be a lie. Do you understand?"

Paul looked at the papers Víctor laid out on the table, took a sip of tea, leaned back in his chair, and said,

"Well, yes, my friend. It's possible. Anything is possible. But still, we have tomorrow."

"Yes, I know. But there's another thing that doesn't sit well with me."

"And what's that?" Paul asked.

"The view from the summit. It's not right. It doesn't match this drawing," Víctor said, worried.

Paul studied the paper closely, pondered for a moment, and then replied,

"If we're relying on a map made from memory—or with the intention to deceive—who knows what's accurate? Go to bed, young man. You'll find out tomorrow regardless. There's no point in worrying about something that's already done. Nothing you think about now will change what happened 186 years ago, or in 1939, or even yesterday."

"Yes, Paul, you're absolutely right about that. Nothing will change, and… tomorrow will be another day."

Chapter XIX

To the Mountain

"Good morning, Diana! Rise and shine! The mountain awaits us!" Víctor called, knocking on her door with a rhythmic rap. He didn't wait for a response—he was too energized to linger. Instead, he headed to the kitchen, eager to start the day.

Most of the group had already gathered around the breakfast table, enjoying coffee, scrambled eggs, bacon, and buttered toast. The only ones missing were Diana and Nina.

"Good morning, everyone! How's Nina?" Víctor asked, taking a seat.

"Good morning," Ashley greeted him with a smile. "She's fine. Slept like a rock. Must've just been exhaustion. Thanks for asking." She glanced toward the hallway. "Diana, on the other hand, still refuses to get up. I called her earlier, and she just groaned and rolled over."

Víctor chuckled. "Yeah, I heard that from my room. That's why I knocked again. She has no escape." He smirked. "She won't miss the big discovery we're going to make today."

Paul, recalling their conversation the night before, leaned back in his chair. "That's the spirit. I see you've woken up full of hope."

"Absolutely, Paul."

Víctor took out the drawing and laid it flat on the table. Turning to Ashley, he tapped a finger on the paper.

"Tell me, what do you see?"

Ashley frowned. "What exactly am I looking for?"

"I'm not sure. Just think back to yesterday, when we were on the hill looking toward Port Louis. Take your time. I'll go check on Diana."

Víctor left as Ashley studied the drawing, turning it in her hands. After a moment, she looked at her parents.

"Do you see anything I don't?" she asked.

Amelia shook her head. "I wasn't on the mountain, remember?"

Paul squinted at the map. "If I compare this to what I remember from yesterday... I'd say something feels off. Maybe it doesn't match."

At that moment, Diana and Víctor returned to the kitchen.

"Mmm, that coffee smells amazing," Diana sighed, running a hand through her hair as she sat down. "Sorry for oversleeping. I was exhausted after yesterday's hike. How embarrassing!"

Ashley waved it off. "Don't worry about it. We're on vacation. Plus, you didn't exactly sign up for this, did you?"

Diana grinned. "Not at all. What an adventure, though. Here we are, solving mysteries. It's wild!"

Ashley smirked. "Yeah, just like Indiana..." she paused dramatically "...or should I say, In-Diana Jones?"

Diana burst into laughter.

Then Ashley turned serious, looking back at Víctor. "I don't know what exactly you're seeing, but I don't think this matches the place we saw yesterday."

She spun the drawing toward Diana. "What do you think? Compare it to the view we had of Port Louis."

Diana studied the paper, silent for a long moment. Víctor held his breath.

Finally, she looked up. "Are we on the wrong mountain?"

The others leaned in as she traced her finger along the sketch.

"Look," she continued, "this bay should be much closer to the mountain, but yesterday we were too far away. Either this drawing is inaccurate... or we were searching in the wrong place entirely."

Paul frowned, rubbing his chin. "But we went to the closest hill north of Port Louis, just like the map suggested. That was the best guess, wasn't it?"

He stood up and went to his desk, returning with a topographical map of the area. Spreading it out on the table, he pointed.

"See? This is where we were."

A wave of unease crept over Víctor. "Then... are you saying..."

Paul hesitated before exhaling. "We were on the wrong mountain or..." he sighed, "and I'm really sorry about this... you're on the wrong island altogether."

Silence.

The words sank in like a stone dropping into deep water. Ashley exchanged a worried glance with Amelia. Diana frowned. Víctor clenched his jaw.

That can't be right, he muttered.

Paul's voice was gentle but firm. "I don't know what to tell you. The geography doesn't match, and if we're wrong about the location…"

"That doesn't make sense," Víctor cut in. His fingers tightened around the edge of the drawing. "We're close. I can feel it."

Before doubt could settle in too deeply, a small voice interrupted them.

"That map is backward."

They turned to see Nina, freshly awake, rubbing her eyes as she crawled onto her mother's lap.

Ashley blinked. "What did you say, sweetheart?"

Nina pointed at the map Víctor was holding up. From her angle, she could see the backside of the paper.

"It's backward," she repeated, yawning. "It's flipped."

A beat of silence hung in the air.

Víctor's breath caught. He grabbed the paper and pressed the front of it against the window, the light shining through. Shadows and lines shifted, revealing a new perspective.

The coastline. The mountains. The layout.

Everything snapped into place.

"Of course... that's it!" He turned to Nina, eyes wide. "You're a genius!".

Paul stepped closer, squinting at the reversed map. His fingers traced the new orientation, his expression shifting from skepticism to astonishment.

"Not only is the map drawn with south at the top..." He exhaled sharply. "It's mirrored."

He pointed to a spot on the map. "These houses here—this isn't Port Louis. It's Johnson's Harbour. And that mountain?" His finger landed on a peak. "North Lookout."

A slow realization settled over them, the weight of discovery pressing in. The map hadn't been misleading them—it had been hiding in plain sight all along.

Víctor's heart pounded. "So that's it, then. We've got it."

Paul nodded. "I'll call David and see what he thinks. That other place is on his land too. We should go there today instead."

Víctor exhaled sharply, a grin spreading across his face. "That's the spot. That's where we'll find it."

Paul, ever the voice of reason, gave him a measured look. "I'm glad you're optimistic. But be careful. Anything is possible—including that this might not be real."

Víctor nodded. "We'll see soon enough."

Paul folded up his map. "At least now, it makes a hell of a lot more sense."

"You know, Paul, why don't we go with them?" Amelia suggested, also excited about it. "Last night, I reread some of Annadee's letters and saw that she mentioned a hill several times as a place they'd go for walks. I had forgotten about that. She doesn't say much else, only that it was the hill by the bay. Could that be significant?"

"It could be," Paul said thoughtfully.

"Don't you see, Paul? This might finally bring closure to Annadee and Patrick's story—or at least help us understand it better. I don't know what will happen today or if we'll find anything, but I hope with all my heart that it's true—that this mystery is finally solved."

"You're right. Why don't you go now?" Paul asked. "I'll join you as soon as I can."

Amelia stood, walked over to Víctor, and said, "Víctor, whatever we think we might find there—maybe it's just an article for your paper or a book—but for me and my family, it's much more than that. I appreciate what you're doing, and I hope you have luck. I hope you're right."

Víctor felt grateful for her words but also deeply worried. He didn't want to disappoint her as he had the day before. In truth, nothing and everything seemed possible.

He exhaled. "I just hope I'm not wrong again, Amelia."

They left the house immediately and set out.

When they arrived at Port Louis, David and Caroline were already waiting for them with everything prepared.

"Good morning," said David. "Paul told me about what you discovered. After searching up there with no results, I started to doubt whether this story of yours was true. But with this new lead, I think we might have better luck today."

"That seems to be the case, David," replied Víctor. "After seeing the site yesterday, I went back to study all the details. Something didn't add up. And thanks to Nina, now we know exactly where we should search. We just have to see what's there."

"Let's hope you're right," added Caroline. "In any case, we'll know the truth today. Have you thought about calling Professor McIntyre, Víctor? I'm sure he'd love to see what we discover."

"I'll call him, but only once we have something solid—when we've found something. No sense in speculating any further."

They checked to ensure they had everything they needed and set out for North Lookout. The location wasn't far—just about fifteen kilometers away—but Víctor didn't want to waste a single moment.

When they reached the settlement of Johnson's Harbour, they turned north, crossed a field of peat bogs, and continued across open ground on a natural animal path. The hill rose about 180 meters, with a gentle incline. As they neared the summit, Víctor began observing the area to decide on the best starting point for their search.

They parked the vehicles as close to the summit as possible, next to one of the tallest rocks. Then, they set up a makeshift camp. Drawing on their experience from the previous day, they organized themselves to thoroughly investigate the site. Caroline and Amelia positioned themselves in the middle; Víctor took the left side with Diana; and David headed for the right flank. From these positions, they imagined a line running along the southern side of the tallest rocks and began walking west.

As they moved, Víctor kept his gaze fixed southward, certain he would recognize a key landmark when he saw it. After walking for a while, he suddenly stopped, his eyes locked on the small settlement of Johnson's Harbour in the distance.

"What is it?" Diana asked. "Do you see something?"

From their vantage point, the entire valley to the south unfolded before them—the slopes stretching toward the cove, the bay glistening beyond, and the mountains forming a rugged backdrop. Víctor scanned the landscape, then pulled the drawing from his pocket, studying it with fresh eyes.

"This is it. Yes, this is definitely it!" he exclaimed, turning to the others as he pointed toward the valley and the settlement. "This is where Karl Henning made his sketch! We've found it!"

The realization struck like a bolt of lightning—the map had been drawn as a mirror image. What appeared on the right in the sketch was actually on the left in reality. It was a deliberate deception, meant to mislead anyone who found it. Nina had been absolutely right.

Now, it was obvious: the settlement Karl had drawn wasn't Port Louis—it was Johnson's Harbour.

"We must be standing right on top of the spot marked with the X. Somewhere here, there's something connected to the *Liberty Rose* and Patrick."

"But I don't see anything," David said, glancing around. "Let me see that drawing."

The others gathered around, comparing the location to the map. The more they studied it, the more certain they became—they had found the right place.

David turned to Víctor, a glimmer of admiration in his eyes. "Looks like you were right. You and Nina."

Amelia and Caroline embraced, excitement bubbling over despite the mystery that still lay ahead.

"Well done, Indy. You did it," Diana teased with a smirk. "You were right all along."

Víctor let out a hearty laugh. "Thanks, Diana. Looks like the trip to the islands was worth it after all."

Caroline crossed her arms. "But… what exactly are we looking for now, Víctor?"

"Oh, well, I'm not sure. Something, I suppose. Maybe a mark, a hidden entrance, something that stands out."

Víctor walked toward the base of one of the large rocks slightly farther north, gesturing for the others to start searching. "Look for anything unusual—a pattern, a marking, something that seems man-made."

After a while, with no luck, David picked up a metal pry bar and began tapping lightly on the rocks, listening for anything out of the ordinary—a hollow sound, a loose stone, a hidden gap. Víctor grabbed another pry bar and did the same.

Suddenly, David, who had been working on the right side of the group, froze. He struck the rock in two different spots, then hit again, harder this time.

"Wait! Come here! Something sounds off!" he called out, tapping again. "Do you hear that?"

Everyone rushed over, listening intently.

"Yes," they answered in unison.

"But we've heard things like that in other spots," Diana pointed out.

David shook his head, tapping again. "Yes, but listen closely. This is different. This is more consistent."

David pressed the pry bar into various spots between the rocks, revealing cavities beneath them.

Víctor stepped back and gestured for everyone to move away from the area. He and David continued tapping, gradually outlining a rough circle. As they worked, David asked Ashley to fetch the spray paint from the toolbox. Once she returned, he used it to mark the boundary between the solid and hollow areas. When they finished, they stepped back and realized they had traced an almost perfect circle about three meters in diameter.

Víctor grabbed a shovel and began clearing the area, removing loose rocks, shrubs, and grass. Soon, a circular formation emerged—massive rocks encircling a center filled with dirt and smaller stones.

His face lit up.

"Are you thinking what I'm thinking?" he asked David.

David nodded. "I think so, Víctor. There's definitely something here."

"I'm calling Paul to let him know," David said, stepping away from the group.

"Good idea. He's going to be thrilled," Caroline added.

Diana, Caroline, and Amelia buzzed with excitement over the discovery, but Víctor urged them to stay calm.

"We still don't know what this is, so let's not celebrate just yet."

"Congratulations anyway, Víctor," Amelia said. "It's obvious there's something here! Everything is starting to make sense."

Víctor smiled. "Thanks, Amelia, but I couldn't have done this alone. So thank you all. Now, we just need to dig."

Amelia stepped closer, placing a hand on Víctor's chest. Meeting his gaze, she spoke softly, "Knowing what's here—what this is—would be incredible, especially for this family. It means so much to us, to me in particular. Thank you."

Víctor shook his head. "There's nothing to thank me for, Amelia. This is just destiny."

As the others went to gather more tools for excavation, Diana and Víctor were left alone for a moment.

"I think I'll cancel my return to Stanley this afternoon," Diana said. "I want to see what's here."

Víctor smiled. "I'm glad to hear that. You shouldn't miss this."

Diana hesitated, then asked, "And you? What are you going to do when you find what you came here for?"

Her tone was laced with uncertainty. Víctor noticed the flicker of sadness in her voice but chose not to acknowledge it. He resisted dwelling on his own emotions.

"I don't know, Diana. We still don't know what's here. It all depends on what we find, of course. Besides, I don't want to keep imposing on these kind people," he said, sidestepping her real question.

"Víctor, you're not imposing," Amelia interjected, having overheard the conversation.

"You're welcome to stay as long as you need."

"Well, thank you, Amelia. That's very kind of you."

Just then, David returned from his phone call.

"Alright, Paul and Ashley are on their way."

"Perfect," said Víctor. "I'll call the professor and update him. He won't believe it. Can I borrow your phone, Diana?"

"Of course."

Víctor stepped aside and made the call. Professor McIntyre answered almost immediately.

"Professor McIntyre, how are you? It's Víctor... Yes, we're doing well—very well. I wanted to let you know we've found something in the field, on a hill. I think we're on the verge of discovering something related to Patrick. Can you come to Johnson's Harbour when you can? To the hill... North Lookout."

"What? You found something? What is it?" the professor asked, his excitement evident.

"We're not sure yet. It's still buried. We need to clear away some stones and dig, but I think this could be a major discovery."

"Oh, wow! I don't even know what to say. That's incredible. Funny enough, I was just about to call you. The lanterns they found definitely belonged to the frigate *Liberty Rose*. There's no doubt about its existence anymore. I've uncovered more information—I'll tell you all about it when we meet. In the meantime, I'll head over as soon as I organize a team and gather my equipment."

"Thank you, Professor. See you soon."

As soon as he ended the call, Víctor returned to the group.

"He's on his way with his team. Let's keep going."

They moved the Rovers closer to the site, arranging them in a semicircle around the marked area to block some of the persistent northwest wind. Using tarps, they secured the space between the vehicles, creating a more sheltered work area. It was now, in effect, an unofficial archaeological site.

"Alright, Indiana Jones," Diana teased. "What's next?"

"David and I will start digging and carefully removing the rocks. Then we'll see what we find."

Carefully, they began moving the stones one by one from the center outward, while the women examined each piece for any markings or clues.

"Do you think these rocks fell from higher up and buried this place, or were they placed here by someone?" Diana asked Víctor.

Víctor studied the formation, then pointed to a massive boulder jutting from the earth, towering nearly six meters above the ground. It tilted southward, directly over the pit.

"Look at how the stones are positioned," he said. "See how it looks like a large piece broke off?"

"Then maybe this isn't the place," Diana reasoned. "It could just be natural—a rockslide, not a man-made pit."

"Maybe, but anything's possible. I still want to keep hoping."

Víctor's confidence wavered after more than an hour of grueling work. They had dug over two meters deep, yet still found nothing. Using pry bars, shovels, and pickaxes, they removed all the loose stones, piling them around the pit's edges as the hole deepened. But there was no sign of anything—just endless rocks and dirt.

Just as they cleared the last of the loose material, Paul, Ashley, and Nina arrived.

"Hey, Mr. Cabot, you were right. Congratulations! I've passed by here a few times—I never would've imagined this," Paul said.

Víctor let out a tired sigh. "Thank you for believing in me and for your help, but... we still haven't found anything. Just rocks and dirt. Nothing. Absolutely nothing." He wiped sweat from his forehead despite the chill in the air. "I know this is the right place, but there's nothing here." He gestured to the pit. "Look, we've hit solid ground. All the loose material is out."

Víctor sat on a protruding rock in the pit wall, his mind racing. Maybe he was in the right area but not the exact spot. Or worse—maybe someone else had already taken whatever had been here.

"Maybe we should try somewhere else. What do you all think?"

"Somewhere else? Where?" David asked, irritation creeping into his voice.

Víctor felt the weight of their expectations. This was the second time he had chosen the wrong location. How much longer would they tolerate his mistakes?

Before anyone could voice their disappointment, he knew he had to act fast. Maybe he had missed something. Maybe he should have searched more thoroughly before committing to a single site.

Frustrated and restless, Víctor leaned forward, jumped down from the ledge, and landed heavily at the bottom of the pit.

The moment his feet touched the ground, the stones beneath him gave way.

With a sudden crack, the earth collapsed. Víctor plunged downward.

A startled cry escaped his lips as he grasped desperately at a crack along the pit's edge. His heart pounded. Beneath him, an abyss yawned—dark, bottomless.

David and Paul lunged toward him but hesitated, afraid their movements might trigger another collapse, dragging Víctor down with it. Loose rocks teetered on the edge, threatening to tumble into the void. The group scrambled to stop them.

"Hold on!" David shouted.

They grabbed one of the ropes they had brought, quickly fashioned a loop at one end, and tossed it down to Víctor, securing the other end to the bumper of one of the Rovers. Víctor slipped the loop over his wrist, then released his grip on the rock, clinging tightly to the rope instead.

With strained effort, the men—joined by the women—hauled him up, hand over hand, until Víctor was safely out of the pit. No one exhaled fully until he was back on solid ground.

Víctor lay there for a moment, catching his breath. "Wow, that was close. Not a great feeling, let me tell you. You saved me. Thank you," he said, still breathing heavily.

Diana knelt beside him, checking for injuries. His hands were scraped, but nothing serious.

"You really gave us a scare," Paul said. "Good thing we were nearby, or we'd have a very different story to tell."

David picked up a flashlight and shone it into the hole, but the beam barely penetrated the darkness.

"Well, as terrifying as that was, I think this is actually good news. I believe we've just found what we're looking for!" Paul exclaimed.

After taking a moment to steady their nerves, they carefully planned how to inspect the hole safely. First, they moved the newly displaced stones farther from the pit to prevent another collapse. Then, they decided to use David's Rover, which was equipped with a front winch, to lower someone down. They positioned the vehicle at a safe distance, unspooled the steel cable, and brought it to the edge of the opening.

Secured to the cable and armed with flashlights, the three men lay on the ground and peered inside.

The entrance—or rather, what had been excavated—resembled a funnel, about three meters wide at the top, narrowing as it descended before transitioning into a vertical shaft that dropped another two meters. At the bottom, a massive cavern opened up, its ceiling stretching high like the vault of a cathedral. A large rock formation jutted out from the entrance, sloping toward the cavern floor.

From their vantage point, they could see directly below, but the deeper recesses of the cavern remained shrouded in shadow. The exposed rock looked smooth and potentially treacherous, with loose debris from the earlier collapse scattered across the floor. One thing was certain—the only way down was to lower someone using the winch.

Víctor, the youngest of the group, stepped forward.

"I'll go first. Once I'm in, I'll make sure it's safe for the rest of you."

They fashioned a makeshift harness from their ropes, securing it around Víctor before hooking him onto the winch. He adjusted his gloves, tugged his wool cap tighter, and took a deep breath. With only a flashlight and his camera, he stepped toward the edge, staring into the abyss below.

"Alright… here goes nothing," he muttered, crouching and sliding forward until he was suspended in the air.

David operated the winch from the Rover while Paul, tied to a safety rope, positioned himself at the edge to oversee the descent.

"Don't leave without me! I'll be back," Víctor joked, flicking on his flashlight.

Paul aimed his own beam downward, tracking Víctor's movement.

As Víctor lowered through the shaft, he adjusted his position, angling the light to scan his surroundings. Shadows twisted and shifted, revealing jagged edges and damp rock. The deeper he descended, the air grew cooler, heavy with the scent of earth, humidity, and time.

Above him, stalactites clung to the ceiling, and the walls curved inward, some sections sloping gently while others dropped off steeply.

He continued his descent until his feet reached a sloped rock midway down. The surface was damp and slick. Carefully, he adjusted his footing, sliding lower until he reached the cavern floor. But as he landed, the loose stones beneath him suddenly shifted, sending him stumbling forward.

Above, Paul lost sight of him but heard the sharp scrape of rock and the clatter of tumbling debris. He instinctively raised a hand, signaling David to stop the winch.

"Víctor! Are you okay? What was that?" Paul shouted.

A tense pause, then Víctor's voice echoed back.

"Yeah... I'm fine... I think so!" he called up. "Just some loose rocks. If I weren't suspended, I probably would've fallen... again."

He steadied himself and shone his flashlight toward the spot where he had stepped. That's when he saw it.

A bone.

It protruded from the pile of fallen stones, and even in the dim light, Víctor knew it was human.

A chill ran down his spine, and for a moment, he was frozen. He swallowed hard, forcing himself to breathe. Then, his beam swept over the area, revealing more bones—partially buried but unmistakable.

His pulse quickened. "Guys! You need to see this!" he shouted. "I think we found someone's remains!"

Stepping carefully over the mound, he scanned the cavern floor. Bones. Scattered, half-buried, some broken. A grim, silent testament to whoever had been trapped here before.

Above, Paul's expression hardened. "Okay, Víctor, wait. I'm coming down too. Is everything safe down there?"

"Hold down, let me check more carefully," Víctor replied. He swept his flashlight across the cavern, taking in its sheer scale.

The chamber was at least thirty meters wide and just as tall. The ceiling arched high, creating an almost dome-like effect. The walls were smooth and slanted toward the entrance—the highest point in the vault. The floor, the flattest and most walkable area, stretched about three meters wide and forty-five meters long, shaped like a semicircle. One wall was concave, the other convex.

Víctor exhaled slowly. A perfect trap. Getting out without a ladder or rope would be nearly impossible.

Víctor continued checking for signs of danger—loose rocks above, hidden pits below—but everything seemed secure.

Then, as he swept his flashlight across the far side of the cave, something glinted in the darkness. He narrowed his eyes and moved toward it. As he got closer, his breath caught.

It was another body. Or rather, what remained of one.

A shiver ran down his spine, though less intensely than before. The shock of the first discovery had braced him for this.

"Hey! There's someone else here!" he called. "Paul, you should come down. It looks safe."

"Alright, on my way."

Víctor unhooked himself from the harness and gave the rope several firm tugs. A moment later, it began retracting as David pulled it up. Víctor then turned back to the skeleton, exhaling slowly as he took in the eerie sight.

The remains were slumped against the cave wall, the skull tilted slightly to one side, as if the person had simply fallen asleep and never woken up. The arms rested on the lap, hands placed one over the other—an eerie gesture of quiet surrender. The legs stretched out before it—one of them clearly broken. They had died there. Alone in the dark.

Víctor sat on a nearby rock, steadying himself. Then, reaching into his pack, he pulled out his camera.

By the time Paul reached the cavern floor, he carried additional flashlights and lanterns. Together, they illuminated the space, positioning the lights strategically to push back the shadows. The steady glow transformed the cave, making the scene before them even clearer.

Beside the skeleton, resting on a rock, lay a tricorn leather hat—the kind worn in the 1700s and early 1800s. Fragments of clothing still clung to the bones: a deteriorated jacket, a shirt, trousers, a wide leather belt, and boots. The leather had preserved remarkably well, the tannins protecting it from total decay.

Near the hat, partially fused into the stone, was a knife. Its blade was corroded with rust, its handle darkened by time.

Paul exhaled sharply. "Do you think it's Patrick?"

Víctor studied the remains, his gaze lingering on the hat. "It could be. The clothing fits the time period. And that hat—it's the right style."

Paul frowned. "Then if this is Patrick... who's under the rocks?"

Víctor hesitated. "Good question, but it has to be Hans... or Karl? They were the only others who seemed to know about this place—besides Patrick.

Maybe they came back here after escaping *Fennia*, and one of them fell."

Paul's expression darkened. "Maybe. But why come back? There's nothing here worth the effort."

Víctor realized Paul was right. There was no obvious reason for them to return. The cave wasn't even a good hiding place—the exit was nearly impossible to reach.

So why?

Determined to find answers, they split up and searched every inch of the cavern. With flashlights in hand, they scoured the space, looking for anything tied to *Liberty Rose* or the treasure from the legend.

They found nothing.

Víctor clenched his jaw. If there had ever been anything here, it was gone.

"One of them..." he murmured, turning to the pile of rocks that concealed the other body. "...took whatever was here."

A voice echoed from above. "You guys okay down there?" David called.

"Yeah, we're fine!" Paul answered. "We're coming up now."

Víctor gave the skeleton one last look. He had come searching for a treasure—but instead, he had solved the disappearance of Patrick Sans McGowan and uncovered the fate of at least one German sailor. That, in the end, felt more valuable than gold.

Paul clapped him on the shoulder. "Let's go. They'll be surprised to hear what we found. Also... I think we should call the police."

They left the lanterns glowing in the darkness. As Paul ascended, Víctor lingered for a moment, lifting his camera and snapping a few final photos.

Then, with a deep breath, he followed Paul up.

As soon as Paul reached the surface, Amelia rushed forward. "What did you find? Who's down there? Is it him?"

Paul nodded. "We believe so. They'll need to run tests—DNA, for confirmation—but we're almost certain."

Víctor climbed up next, and Amelia immediately turned to him, repeating the same questions. But instead of answering, Víctor simply reached into his pocket and pulled out the knife he had found beside the skeleton.

The group fell silent as he uncapped a water bottle and began washing away the layers of dirt and time. He rubbed the handle with his jacket sleeve, revealing hints of silver and gold beneath the patina. Slowly, letters emerged, etched deep into the metal.

The moment the name became clear, gasps filled the air.

"Patrick Sans McGowan."

Amelia stepped closer, her hands trembling as she took the knife. Her fingers brushed over the name, as if touching it would somehow bring him back. Her breath hitched, her eyes glistening as tears slipped down her cheek."

"Oh, no. It can't be..." Her voice was barely above a whisper. "Annadee—my Annadee—she searched for him her whole life. She never stopped. And all this time, he was here?"

Víctor swallowed hard. "It seems so, Amelia. I... I'm so sorry. For them, for you, for the family."

Paul cleared his throat gently. "To be absolutely certain, we still need to investigate further."

Amelia barely heard him. She was still staring at the knife.

"There's someone else down there, too," Víctor added.

Caroline tensed. "Who?"

"We don't know yet. But it must be one of the German prisoners." He exhaled, glancing at Paul. "We haven't moved the rocks covering him, but from what we can see, the clothing is better preserved—much more recent than Patrick's. It looks like a cave-in crushed him. But Patrick... he must have fallen, broken his leg, and gotten trapped. There was no way out without help from above."

Caroline crossed her arms. "And *Liberty Rose*? Did you find anything from the ship?"

Víctor shook his head. "No. There is nothing else down there—if it was, it's gone now."

Caroline frowned. "But then how did Henning know about the ship? It's in his drawings."

Paul sighed. "That's the real mystery now. But the truth is, whatever was left... isn't there anymore."

A heavy silence settled over them.

Amelia turned to Caroline, still clutching the knife. "Do you realize what this means? Annadee died believing he abandoned her. She spent her whole life thinking he left... we all did. But in reality, he was here, all this time. All these years."

Caroline's eyes softened. She reached out, squeezing Amelia's hand before pulling her into an embrace. "I know. And now, at least, we can finally understand what happened. We can give him peace. And you too."

Nearby, Diana, Ashley, and Nina exchanged stunned glances, their faces reflecting a mix of awe and sorrow.

Amelia took a deep breath, steadying herself. Then, with quiet resolve, she said, "We'll take him to Stanley. He should be buried alongside Annadee and their daughter. That's where he belongs."

Paul nodded. "Of course, Honey. Once we've finished everything here, I'll take care of it."

David called the Stanley police to report their discovery. Afterward, the group decided to head back down and start clearing the rocks covering the other body.

"I don't mean to ruin the moment, but... shouldn't we wait for the police? This could be a crime scene," Diana hesitated.

David shrugged. "Nah, I don't think they'll mind. We're just speeding up their work."

"We're only reopening a closed case," Víctor added. "And honestly, this looks more like an accident than anything else."

Paul and David descended first, leaving Caroline and Amelia to manage the winch above. Víctor followed, finding the others standing silently by Patrick's remains.

Not wanting to interrupt, he knelt and started carefully removing the stones from the second body. After a moment, the others joined him, working methodically, eager for answers but careful not to damage what lay beneath. Some of the rocks were massive, weighing up to twenty kilos—whoever had been trapped there never stood a chance. The good news was that the cavern now seemed stable.

As they worked, they uncovered the body face down, its head pointed away from the entrance—as if it had once been lying on its stomach when the collapse happened or had tumbled forward, sliding down the sloped wall before being crushed. A length of rope was still wrapped around part of the torso.

David, closest to the head, reached under the neck, searching for a military identification tag—proof that he is one of the prisoners that escaped *Fennia*. His flashlight caught the glint of metal. Carefully, he pulled out a oval dog tag, brushing away dust and debris until the inscription became clear:

> "Kriegsmarine A
> Hans Schneider
> N 4778/39 K"

A heavy silence settled over them.

Víctor exhaled. "That confirms it." His theories had been correct—everything was falling into place.

Then Paul, working near the legs, froze.

"Wait a minute," he said, his voice tight with surprise. "I think there's someone else here. I see… another hand."

"What?" The others rushed over.

With renewed urgency, they cleared away more stones. Slowly, another figure emerged.

Like the first, this one wore the same style of clothing, confirming that both were the German sailors who had escaped from the *Fennia*. Like the other, this body has the metal dog tag still hanging from to the neck—which was slightly bent from the weight of the rocks. The inscription read:

"Kriegsmarine B
Karl Henning
54879/39 K"

Seventy-eight years had passed since their escape.

Karl lay face down, his head pointed in the opposite direction from Hans Schneider's. His hands were over his head, his body arched—as if he had tried to shield himself from the collapse.

Then, as they shifted the last of the rocks, they realized something else.

Beneath Karl, trapped between his stomach and the cavern floor, was a chest.

For a moment, no one moved.

Then, as if breaking free from a trance, Víctor whispered, "Could it be...?"

Their exhaustion vanished in an instant. Carefully, they lifted Karl's remains, treating them with the respect they deserved, though their growing excitement was impossible to ignore.

Meanwhile, Ashley and Diana descended into the cavern, drawn first to Patrick's resting place. In the soft glow of the lantern beside him, he seemed to watch over everything—silent, eternal. Paul and David soon joined them, standing in quiet reverence.

Víctor, however, remained focused. Kneeling beside the chest, he brushed away layers of dust and turquoise-green patina, his gloved fingers moving carefully over the surface. Faint lettering emerged. He wiped again, and this time, the name became unmistakable:

"Liberty Rose."

A sharp breath escaped him.

"Yes! It's still here!" His voice echoed off the cavern walls.

At last, they had found it. Patrick Sans McGowan. Hans Schneider. Karl Henning. And the lost chest of the *Liberty Rose*. Just as Annadee had written in her journal. Just as Karl had marked on the map. It had all been true.

The others, after their quiet moment with Patrick, gathered around.

Ashley, unable to resist, reached for the chest's lid. She tried to lift it—but it wouldn't budge.

"It's stuck," she muttered.

Paul grabbed a rock and gently tapped along the edges.

Ashley tried again and the lid gave way.

The moment it opened, a collective gasp filled the cavern.

Paul exhaled in awe. "This is incredible."

Chapter XX

1939
Hidden Atop North Lookout Hill

After a few hours, as night fell and the moon rose on the horizon, they began to move in the dim light. Karl went first. He climbed onto the rock that had served as his hiding spot and slid down its slanted surface like a makeshift slide. As he did, part of the rock crumbled beneath him, causing him to slip and land heavily on the ground, which was covered in loose stones. The sudden noise caught their attention.

"Hans, what was that?"

"I don't know. It sounded weird... hollow. Be careful. Let me take a look."

Karl started to get up, but before he could steady himself, the ground beneath him gave way. In an instant, he was swallowed into the darkness.

Everything happened so fast—there was no time to react, no chance to scream.

What the hell just happened? What is this? Karl muttered as his abrupt descent ended at the bottom of a cavern.

Hans, unable to see clearly in the darkness, hesitated at the edge of the pit.

"Hey," Hans whispered. "Are you alright? Can you hear me?"

"Yeah," Karl shouted back. "I think I've hit the bottom. It looks like the pit ends here."

He scrambled to his feet, trying to make sense of his surroundings.

"*Scheisse!* That scared me!"

He tried to climb the slanted wall he had just slid down to the bottom. It was impossible.

"Hans, I don't think I can get out! I can't!" Karl called, his voice tinged with rising panic.

"Hold on. I'll lower the flashlight. Maybe you can find a way to climb out or spot another exit."

Hans quickly tied the flashlight to the rope, switched it on, and lowered it into the pit.

As the cave illuminated, an eerie sensation crept over Karl.

He wasn't alone.

A cold shiver ran down his spine as he turned his head, scanning the shadows. Then he saw it.

It wasn't the skeleton itself that unsettled him—he had seen death up close too many times. What disturbed him was the mystery of how and why someone had been left to rot in such a place.

Would he meet the same fate?

For a moment, he forgot about their mission. Forgot about time.

"Well, Karl, what do you see?" Hans asked, his voice tinged with concern.

Karl swallowed hard. "There's… a skeleton down here."

"What? Well, it's already dead, right?" Hans replied, unimpressed. "Leave it alone, let's go."

Karl, however, felt more curiosity than a sense of urgency to escape. He untied the flashlight from the rope and stepped closer to investigate. He and the dead man shared this cavern now—that much was certain. And he wasn't leaving without understanding who this person had been and why they had ended up here.

"What happened to you, my friend? Why are you here?" Karl murmured, pitying the long-forgotten figure. "Were you left here? Did they abandon you?"

His eyes caught something nearby. Resting on a stone beside the skeleton was a rusted flintlock pistol and a knife with a silver-and-gold hilt. Despite the dampness, the knife's handle had remained intact.

Wiping the hilt clean with his shirt, Karl revealed an engraved name:

Patrick Sans McGowan.

He realized that this man had been down here for decades. Maybe even longer.

The skeleton sat hunched forward, resting on its legs. Karl carefully grasped its shoulders and head, easing it back with surprising gentleness. He handled it as if it were still alive, careful not to disturb what time had already eroded. The bones, held together by fragments of cartilage and the tattered remains of clothing, told a silent story. Judging by the unnatural angle of one leg, the man had suffered a brutal break.

As he carefully shifted the skeleton, something else emerged—a wooden chest with copper plating, tarnished by age. Carved into its surface was a name: Liberty Rose.

What had Patrick been protecting so desperately? he questioned himself.

Karl unhooked the rusted padlock and pried open the lid.

Coins. Gold and silver ingots. A gold cross encrusted with emeralds gleamed in the dim light.

He couldn't believe it.

He was rich.

Rich. But trapped in a cave. Unable to climb out. Far from home. In the middle of a war. On an enemy island, in the middle of the ocean.

What an irony, he thought.

"Hans! Hans! You won't believe this! Look what I found!" Karl shouted.

"Hey, Karl, I'm right here. Stop yelling. Hurry up, we have to leave."

"Hans, look! A chest full of gold! Can you believe it? A treasure!"

Karl glanced back at the skeleton and muttered, *I guess you won't be needing this anymore, my friend.*

He closed the lid, hooked the padlock back into place, and dragged the chest toward the rope.

"Hans, we're rich! Do you hear me? We're rich! We have to get this out of here!"

Hans hesitated, staring at him from above. "Are you delirious, Karl? Did that fall knock something loose? What the hell are you talking about?"

Then his voice dropped to a whisper. "Listen, I saw lights. Someone's approaching the village. We need to leave. Now."

"But look at this, Hans!" Karl's voice brimmed with excitement.

"Gold coins, a crucifix with emeralds! I'll tie it to the rope—pull it up!" Hans grabbed the rope and started to lift it but then stopped halfway.

"Wait. Hold on, Karl. Think for a second. Where are we going to take this? We're in enemy territory. At war. And we haven't even made it out of here yet, we don't even know the condition of that sailboat."

Karl frowned. "What are you saying? Don't you get it? This is our way out—our freedom! We can go anywhere and buy our own boat!"

Hans exhaled sharply. "Listen, let's think this through. We leave it here and come back when it's safe. What do you think will happen if they find us with that? If it's been down here this long, it'll still be here when the war's over. Carrying this will slow us down and put us at risk. Do you want to be free or not?"

Karl hated to admit it—but Hans was right.

"Well, maybe you do have a better head on your shoulders than I do. I think, yes, it's a good idea," he said. "The war will be over soon, and we'll be able to return in peace."

Hans lowered the chest, Karl untied it, carefully placing it beside the skeleton.

"Goodbye, Herr Patrick Sans McGowan. At least now I know your name. We'll see each other soon. Take care of this. We'll come back for it."

Then he took the rope that Hans was holding, tied it around his chest and underarms, and climbed up the wall. Once at the top, they covered the cave, making sure it was well concealed so that no one else would find it.

"I hope you're right, Hans. That must be worth a fortune. It worries me to just leave it like this. I just hope we can get it back."

"Of course we will. Soon. You'll see," Hans said

Without wasting time, they turned their attention to the village. While Karl had been in the cave, someone had arrived. Now, a truck was parked in front of one of the houses, its lights on inside, though no people were visible.

After waiting a bit, they decided to stick to the plan. They couldn't wait any longer. If they sailed all night, by the time anyone noticed the sailboat missing, they'd be far away. The Argentine coast awaited them, and Argentina wasn't at war with Germany. They'd have better chances there.

The moon was high on the horizon, clearly illuminating the path they needed to follow from the mountain. They calculated it would take about half an hour to cover the two kilometers to the village and board the sailboat, finally sailing toward their freedom. They gathered everything they had, leaving no trace behind, made sure the cave was well concealed, and left their hideout.

The plan was to skirt the village on the left, keeping away from the bay, pass the village entirely, and then head straight for the dock.

Moving swiftly and in silence, they descended the hill, their eyes locked on the inhabited house. One wrong move, and everything would be lost.

As they neared their target, faint voices in English reached their ears. They froze, crouching lower, their bodies tense. Moving cautiously, they weaved through the thick tussock grass, using the cover it provided. A small hill obscured their view of the dock, but they knew the way—pass between the first houses and the shed, and they'd be there. Seeing no lights and no movement, they paused, scanning the area one last time before stepping into the open.

Hunched over and utterly silent, they crept nearly 200 meters, their breaths shallow, their eyes locked on the sailboat glistening under the moonlight. Freedom was within their grasp.

Then a voice shattered the night.

"Stop! You're surrounded!"

A dozen marines with rifles emerged from the shed and the nearby house, cutting off their escape. There was no point in resisting. No chance to run. Slowly, they raised their hands. The dice of fate had been cast.

The soldiers searched them, stripping away everything but their clothes, then loaded them into a truck hidden in the shed.

They never suspected that they were walking straight into a trap.

While they had been busy escaping the cave, they hadn't noticed that with the truck had also come a military transport with a royal marine troop.

The ride was long and silent. When they finally arrived, the truck rumbled through the deserted streets of a larger town before stopping at the harbor entrance. There, a large sailing ship stood waiting, guarded by sentries.

It was the *Fennia*.

At dawn, they were brought before a group of officers for questioning. They had little to say—only the truth of what had happened and how they had ended up there. The war had only just begun. There wasn't much else to know.

After the interrogation ended, they were taken back to *Fennia.*

Once their nerves had settled, they gathered at the bow of the ship and lit a cigarette they'd managed to get from one of the guards.

"How did they treat you, Karl?"

"Well enough. I didn't know much, and that's all I said. I think they believed me."

"Yeah, same here. The war's over for me. In fact, this war was never mine to begin with. Hitler's insane. But we were just following orders, weren't we?"

"Yeah, we were," Hans muttered.

From the bow, nearly all of Stanley was visible. The cascade of neatly arranged houses along the hillside presented a peaceful, orderly, and tranquil scene.

"Look at this town, Hans. It'd be a nice place to settle down here, don't you think?"

"Maybe, but I'll take Germany. Fewer enemies there," Hans said with a smile. "Did you hear they're saying we'll be sent to South Africa soon, with the others?"

"Yeah, that's what they're saying. But we'll have to come back here anyway—don't forget we have something hidden. Do you remember where we left it?" Karl said

"Well… kind of. My mind was on escaping and getting you out of that pit, not so much on the treasure. How about you? Think we can find it again?"

"I think so. I'm good at that. What do you think happened to him? Why was he there?"

"I'm not sure. Maybe the guy fell, like you did. What do you think, Karl?"

"Well, it looks like he fell—or maybe he was pushed—and with his leg broken, he couldn't climb out. Poor man. I was lucky you were there and that we brought the ropes from the boat, Hans. Although, thinking about it, if I hadn't come out, maybe we'd still be on the mountain and not prisoners. Hmm, nothing would've worked out either way."

Hans simply stared at the horizon, taking slow drags from his cigarette without saying anything.

"I'm going to write a letter to my family. There's so much to tell. Today's Saturday; the Red Cross will collect the letters on Wednesday and deliver them. Did the captain tell you that? You should write one. Make good use of the time. Your family must be worried if they've already heard about the sinking."

"You're right. I'll finish this cigarette and head down to write. Christmas is on Monday—I think we'll spend it here. Honestly, I hope we stay here until this damned war is over."

Just as the prisoners had been speculating, activity started aboard the *HMS Cumberland* that day. It looked like they were preparing the ship for departure.

If not for what they'd found on that mountain, they might not have cared as much. But the uncertainty of what would happen next left them with a bitter taste. That treasure seemed far too valuable to leave behind. So, they started to plan. They had to find a way to return to that cave, retrieve the treasure, and escape to Argentina, just as they had originally intended. They didn't know how or when, but they'd figure it out.

Chapter XXI

2017
North Lookout Hill

Inside the old trunk lay the treasure Patrick had once discovered.

For a moment, no one spoke. They simply exchanged stunned glances, searching for an explanation, struggling to process what they had just uncovered.

Ashley was the first to recover from the shock. Carefully, she began removing each item, one by one. First, a golden cross adorned with massive emeralds, attached to a thick gold chain nearly a meter long. Then, six gold ingots, six silver ingots, twenty-two gold coins, and seventeen silver coins. At the bottom, they found a stack of fragile papers, their edges crumbling with age. They decided not to touch them—for now.

Víctor quickly snapped some photos before they carefully returned everything to the chest.

"What do you think all this is worth?" Paul asked.

Ashley exhaled, her eyes fixed on the treasure. "Dad, this treasure cost at least three people their lives—and who knows how many others? Not to mention Annadee's suffering. How can you possibly put a price on that?"

A heavy silence settled over them.

Then, Amelia's voice broke through from above, tense with urgency. "Guys! Several vehicles are coming down the road!"

Víctor turned to Paul. "Good, they are coming. What's going to happen with all of this?"

"Good question," Paul said, "I've never found a treasure before. How would I know?"

David crossed his arms. "Well, it's on my property. But we only found it thanks to you, Víctor. And then there's the matter of the *Liberty Rose*. Who did it really belong to? What flag did it sail under? Patrick discovered it, but no one ever claimed it."

Víctor nodded. "The professor might have some answers. He told me he had news about the ship. He'll be thrilled when he sees all this."

Paul sighed. "This could get complicated, especially with the remains of those prisoners of war we found."

"Or," Víctor countered, "it might finally shed light on what happened to them—and why there's so little information about the *SMS Kielberg*. There were rumors of a secret mission. At the very least, this could bring closure to their families… as it did to yours, Paul. If those men were listed as missing or killed in action, their families deserve to know the truth."

Paul gave a small, knowing smirk. "Another opportunity for a new story, Mr. Cabot? Perhaps you should stay around these parts, don't you think?" Víctor smiled and nodded. The idea clearly excited him. There was no shortage of stories to research, uncover, and write about—and, of course, Diana.

Víctor stepped away from the group, who remained talking about the discovery and the treasure they had unearthed. Looking at the full scene—the evidence in plain view, the recounted stories, Karl's letters, and the map—he pieced together what had happened to Patrick Sans McGowan and the fate of the prisoners of war.

He used the moment to take more photos of the site and the remains. Then he gazed at everything, forming a theory.

"Friends, I think what happened here is obvious. You may have already figured it out too. Want to hear my theory?" he asked.

"Of course."

"This cavern has probably existed since the islands were formed—it's consistent with lava bubbles or tectonic shifts. I'm sure the professor can give us a better explanation. Anyway, Patrick hid the chest in that pit up there and covered it. When he returned to retrieve it to flee with Annadee aboard the *USS Lexington*, he dug it out and removed the stones. I think the extra weight of the stones he used to seal it, combined with his own weight when he went down for the chest, caused the floor of the pit—the roof of this cavern—to give way. Just like what happened to me. When he fell from up there, he broke his leg—that's obvious. We know he survived the fall for at least some time. I'm sure he must have shouted for help, but no one heard him. His horse probably ran off, startled by the collapse, and if someone found it, they either didn't report it or stole it. Who knows? Remember the chaos of that time. That same collapse must have blocked the entrance for a long time.

Then, 107 years later, in 1939, Karl and Hans came through here while fleeing after their ship sank. We don't know exactly what happened, but they must have found this place before being captured and taken prisoner. On the *Fennia*, they created the map in case they couldn't return immediately—perhaps fearing they would forget the location. When they escaped, they returned here and tried to retrieve the chest, planning to sail, I assume, to Argentina. My guess is Karl descended into the pit, aided by Hans with the rope. Karl managed to tie up the chest, but when Hans tried to lift it, part of the roof where Hans stood gave way. He fell, bringing stones down with him. Both likely died instantly, and the same movement of rocks blocked the entrance again. That's why no one else found them. Not until now, when we arrived."

"Well, that's a theory that makes sense," Ashley said.

"I'm glad our wives are up there to help if there's another collapse," Paul joked. "Still, I think we'd better get out of here as soon as possible."

"Yes, let's go," David agreed.

"We'll leave everything as is for the police and the professor to examine."

One by one, they climbed out.

Epilogue

One hundred and eighty-five years had passed since the disappearance of Patrick Sans McGowan, and 78 years since the escape and vanishing of German Navy Sergeant Hans Schneider and sailor Karl Henning. Two unsolved mysteries had finally been solved.

Professor McIntyre arrived with his archaeological team, followed later by several police officers, accompanied by Lieutenant James Wilkinson.

After an initial investigation, the site was cordoned off, and an officer was assigned to guard it overnight.

The next day, after the survey and police investigation were complete, they carefully retrieved the chest and began the solemn task of removing the remains. One by one, the past was unearthed—silent witnesses to a story long buried. Patrick's remains were the last to be brought out, an emotional reminder of a fate sealed by choices made long ago.

The police report on the prisoners of war was sent to naval authorities for a more thorough investigation. The bodies of the German sailors were taken to the morgue at Stanley Hospital, where DNA records were processed to confirm their identities. The condition of the bodies indicated that the collapse was what had killed them. They were buried in the local cemetery, awaiting potential claims from their families.

A DNA test confirmed Patrick's identity, and on July 15—the very day he first set foot in the

Falkland Islands aboard the brig *Elbe*—he was laid to rest beside Annadee and their daughter, Patricia. At last, they were together.

In his casket, Amelia placed the letters his beloved Annadee had written to him. The exact cause of his death could not be determined, but he had a fractured left leg and three broken ribs. All they could do was imagine how long he had survived in that cave, succumbing to his injuries, thirst, hunger, and the desperation of being trapped. Studies conducted by the police and Professor McIntyre's team determined that Patrick had fallen into the cave around the same time he disappeared. The same happened with Hans and Karl.

The treasure found in the chest had belonged to the frigate *Liberty Rose*, but nothing more was discovered about the origin or intended use of its contents. The papers in the chest were set aside for further study. They appeared to be orders for research and exploration. It is believed the frigate was attacked by privateers or pirates, its crew killed or lost at sea, and the ship left adrift sometime between September and December of 1831. The treasure was divided equally between its discoverer and the landowner, in accordance with the law, since no official claims were made, and no origin marks were found.

The gold-and-emerald cross with its chain is now one of the main attractions of the Stanley Museum, along with Patrick's knife.

The cavern was sealed off to prevent further accidents.

As for Víctor, he stayed on the islands for Patrick's burial. He wanted to be there when he was given a Christian burial. He also attended the burials of Karl Henning and Hans Schneider.

On that gray day, after the funerals ended, Diana and Víctor made their way down the long cemetery staircase to the street. Despite the cold, they sat on the final steps, sheltered from the wind by a low retaining wall, while the others said their goodbyes and departed. Suddenly, everything grew silent, everything slowed down, and life paused for a moment—even the wind.

"It's over, Víctor. No more secrets from the *Fennia*," Diana said, resting her hand on his knee.

Víctor exhaled, his breath visible in the crisp air. "It seems that way. I never imagined where that box would take me."

Diana gave a small smile. "Life is full of surprises. The question is—what do we do with them?"

Víctor sighed. "Yes, I know. But look at Patrick—he went back for his treasure and got trapped. If he had just boarded the ship with Annadee, things would have been different. He was so young. They had a whole life ahead of them. Was the treasure really worth more than their happiness? And Hans and Karl... they had their freedom. They could have escaped to Argentina, but they returned for the chest—and lost their lives because of it."

He gazed toward the horizon. "How often do we set our own traps? Temptations that seem easy to resist but quietly ensnare us. How many times have we traded true happiness for the illusion of something greater—something that, in the end, was never worth it?"

Diana didn't answer. Instead, she leaned in and pressed a gentle kiss to his lips, and he returned it just as softly. Turning away, she rested her head against his chest, seeking his warmth. He wrapped his arm around her, pulling her closer as their fingers intertwined.

They sat in silence, watching the horizon. There was nothing left to say.

In the distance, fishing boats rocked gently in the bay, swaying with the unrelenting rhythm of the waves—waiting patiently for their next journey to sea.